Temple Prime

Descent of Comfort Sands and of his Children

with notes on the families of Ray, Thomas, Guthrie, Alcock, Palgrave,

Cornell, Dodge, Hunt, Jessup

Temple Prime

Descent of Comfort Sands and of his Children
with notes on the families of Ray, Thomas, Guthrie, Alcock, Palgrave, Cornell, Dodge, Hunt, Jessup

ISBN/EAN: 9783337267698

Printed in Europe, USA, Canada, Australia, Japan

Cover: Foto ©Andreas Hilbeck / pixelio.de

More available books at **www.hansebooks.com**

DESCENT

OF

COMFORT SANDS

AND OF

HIS CHILDREN,

WITH NOTES ON THE FAMILIES OF

RAY,	ALCOCK,	DODGE,
THOMAS,	PALGRAVE,	HUNT,
GUTHRIE,	CORNELL,	JESSUP.

NEW YORK
1886

The undersigned, in publishing this memorandum in its present form (i. e., of proof-sheets), has in view a twofold object: first, to preserve from destruction, notes, the result of much trouble and research; secondly, to court criticism and to elicit further information.

At some no distant time the undersigned is in hopes of republishing this matter in a somewhat more complete shape.

T. P.

New York, 1886.

SANDS.

JAMES I SANDS.

Born: in England, 1622.
Died: on Block Island, March 13th 1695; interred there.*
Married: in England? Sarah (Walker?); will dated October 17th 1703; on record on Block Island.
Will: June 18th 1694; on record on Block Island.

Issue.

1. **John I Sands,** of whom later.
2. **Edward Sands,** settled on Block Island, married there, and had one daughter, Sarah, who married Teddi-

---

*Buried in the public graveyard; the stone over his remains, a large recumbent sandstone slab, still in a good state of preservation, bears the following inscription:

"Here Lyes In
Tvrred the Body
of Mr. James Sands,
Seniovr aged 73
Years departed
This life March
The 13 1695."

man Hull, of Block Island; died on Block Island, June 14th 1708; interred alongside of his father.*

3. **Samuel Sands,** born *circa* 1656, removed to Cowneck, Queens Co., N. Y., in 1696; married 1679 a daughter of Simon II Ray of Block Island, a sister to the wife of his brother John I Sands; died 1730; he and his wife were interred on his farm at Cowneck; he left one son.

4. **Sarah Sands,** married on Block Island, February 14th 1671, Nathaniel Niles; left issue.

5. **James II Sands,** born on Block Island, *circa* 1662; removed to Matinicock, L. I., 1696; married 1697, Mary, daughter of John I Cornell, of Cowneck; died 1731; will dated September 21st 1730; interred on his farm; left issue male.

6. **Mercy Sands,** born on Block Island; married April 29th 1683, Joshua Raymond; removed 1704 to New London, Conn.

Account of James I Sands.

Came from England, and, as tradition has it, from Reading, Berkshire; landed at Plymouth, Mass.; 1642 engaged in building a house for Mrs. Hutchinson at Eastchester, Westchester Co., N. Y.; removed to Portsmouth, R. I., in which place he had grants of land October 5th 1643, and August 29th 1644; 1655 freeman at Portsmouth, R. I.; May 19th 1657 commissioner from Portsmouth at the General Court; April 1661 he and his family sailed

---

*Buried in the public graveyard; the stone over his remains, a large recumbent sandstone slab, still in a good state of preservation, bears the following inscription:

"Here lyeth interred
The body of Captⁿ
Edward Sands who
Departed this life Jvne
Ye 14 1708 in ye. . .
Yeare of his age."

from Taunton, Mass., for Block Island, on which they settled;* March 1663-4 constable on Block Island; 1665 deputy from Block Island; October 1670 and September 1671 tax-rater on Block Island; November 15th 1690 he made a deed to his son, John I Sands, of the land upon which he settled, when he first landed on Block Island.

JOHN I SANDS.

Born: in America, 1649.

Died: on the Home Farm,† Cowneck, L. I., March 15th 1712; interred ‡ on Cowneck, in the Sands graveyard.

Married: on Block Island, Sybil, daughter of Simon II Ray; § born 1665, died on Cowneck, December 23d 1733; interred ‖ alongside of her husband; intestate.

Will: intestate.

---

* In 1808 the land on which he first settled was held and occupied by a descendant, one John Sands; the homestead on Block Island, in which he lived and died, and which he left to his son, Edward Sands, was held by descendants of the name of Hull.

† See page 20.

‡ His gravestone, which is upright, and still in good condition, has on it the following inscription:

> "Here lieth ye Body
> of John Sands
> Died March ye 15th
> 1712 In ye 63d
> Year of his age."

§ For an account of the Ray family see page 40.

‖ Her gravestone of slate, and upright, and still in good condition, bears the following inscription:

> 'Here lieth ye Body
> Of Sibell ye wife
> Of John Sands
> Died Decem. ye 23
> 1733 In ye 68:
> Year of her age."

Issue.

1. **John II Sands,** of whom later.
2. **Nathaniel Sands,** born on Block Island 1687; died May 10th 1750; line extinct.
3. **Edward Sands,** born 1691, settled on Cowneck, L. I.; died March 9th 1746; left issue male.
4. **George Sands,** born on Cowneck 1694; died unmarried; interred in the Sands graveyard on Cowneck.
5. **Dorothy Sands,** born 1703; died 1765; married —— Bowne.
6-8. Three daughters.

Account of John I Sands.

1674 May 27th had a grant of land in Portsmouth, R. I.

1678, 80 and 81 Deputy to the General Assembly from Block Island.

1691 removed from Block Island to Cowneck, L. I. and purchased a farm* of Richard Cornell of Rockaway, deed dated December 25th 1691, this farm was included in a patent taken out by Cornell in 1686, consideration £200; the farm of his brother Samuel, adjoining this one, was a part of the land purchased; he gave his descendants a graveyard of about half an acre immediately north of his house; he left the Home Farm to his son Nathaniel, his widow remaining on the same until her death.

---

* See page 20.

JOHN II SANDS.

Born: on Block Island, January 22d 1683-84.

Died: on the Home Farm Cowneck, August 15th 1763; interred * in the Sands graveyard.

Married: at Newport, R. I., September 9th 1706, Catherine, daughter of Robert Guthrie; † born on Block Island June 24th 1690; died on Cowneck February 10th 1769; interred ‡ alongside of her husband; intestate.

Will: February 27th 1759; proved September 30th 1763; recorded in the Surrogate's Office, N. Y., Liber 24, fol. 224.

Issue.

1. **John III Sands,** of whom later.
2. **Robert Sands,** born on Block Island, December 26th 1710; died unmarried, April 12th 1735; interred on Cowneck.
3. **Edward Sands,** born on Block Island, January 17th 1711-12; died October 21st 1778; ancestor of all the Sands at present on Block Island.
4. **Mary Sands,** born 1715; died March 15th 1724.
5. **George Sands,** born 1717; died unmarried January 15th 1777; interred on Cowneck.

---

* His gravestone, of sandstone, and upright, and still in good condition, bears the following inscription:
"In
Memory of
John Sands
The 2d who departed this
Life August 30th 1763.
Aged 79 years."

† For an account of the Guthrie family see page 54.

‡ Her gravestone, of sandstone, and upright, and still in good condition, bears the following inscription:
"In
Memory of
Catherine Sands
Relict of John Sands the 2d
Who departed this life
February 10th 1769.
Aged 78 years."

6. **Anne Sands,** born March 16th 1719; married —— Brooks.

7. **Nathaniel Sands,** born November 30th 1721; died August 1783; left issue male.

8. **Joshua Sands,** born March 22d 1725; died March 28th 1787; left issue male.

9. **Simon Sands,** born July 12th 1727; died April 5th 1782; left issue male.

10. **Gideon Sands,** born October 22d 1729; died April 20th 1770; left issue male; interred on Cowneck.

11. **Mary Sands,** born 1732; married —— Guilford; died February 19th 1755.

12. **Benjamin Sands,** born November 1735; died October 14th 1824; left issue male.

Account of John II Sands.

He lived on Block Island until about ten years after his marriage and then moved to a farm in the interior of Cowneck, where he built a house and remained until about 1733, when he removed to the Home Farm, which he had purchased from his brother Nathaniel.

JOHN III SANDS.

Born : on Block Island, January 1st 1708–09.

Died : on the Inland Farm, Cowneck, November 22d 1760; interred * in the Sands graveyard.

---

* His gravestone, of sandstone, and upright, and still in good condition, bears the following inscription:

"Here
Lies the Body
Of
John Sands,
Who departed this life,
November the 22d 1760,
Aged 51 years."

Married: May 12th 1736, Elizabeth, daughter of Caleb I Cornell;* born September 27th 1711; died May 10th 1793; interred † by her husband; intestate.

Will: October 9th 1760; proved December 12th 1760; recorded in the Surrogate's Office, N. Y., Liber 22, fol. 363.

Issue.

1. **John IV Sands,** born February 22d 1737; died June 25th 1811; left issue male.

2. **Cornwell Sands,** born April 26th 1739; died August 3d 1793; left no issue male.

3. **Elizabeth Sands,** born May 8th 1742; died September 13th 1747.

4. **Robert Sands,** born February 13th 1745; died March 8th 1825; left no issue male.

5. **Comfort Sands,** of whom later.

6. **Stephen Sands,** born January 16th 1750; died January 31st 1787; left issue male.

7. **Richardson Sands,** born June 13th 1754; left issue male.

8. **Joshua Sands,** ‡ born October 12th 1757; died September 13th 1835; left issue male.

Account of John III Sands.

Settled on the Inland Farm 1733; all his children were born there; he died there and his widow also; after his death the farm passed to his eldest son John IV Sands.

---

* For account of the Cornell family see page 69.

† Her gravestone, of sandstone, and upright, and still in good condition, bears the following inscription:

"Here
Lies the body of
Elizabeth Sands,
The wife of John Sands, who
Departed this life May the 10th
1793, aged 81 years 7 months
and 13 days."

‡ There is a portrait of him in the Long Island Historical Society, Brooklyn, presented by the family.

COMFORT SANDS.

Born: on the Inland Farm on Cowneck. February 26th 1748; baptized in St. Paul's Chapel, New York, in the summer of 1767.

Died: Hoboken, N. J., September 22d 1834; interred.*

Will: 5th January 1833; proved 5th May 1836; recorded in the Surrogate's Office, N. Y., Liber 75, fol. 78.

Married: 1st. At Hunt's Point, Westchester Co. by the Rev. Samuel Seabury, Rector of Westchester, later Bishop of Connecticut, June 3d 1769, Sarah, daughter of Wilkie I Dodge;† born at Hunt's Point 1749; died New York January 24th 1795; interred‡§ in her husband's vault in the Middle Dutch Church, Nassau street; intestate.

———— 2dly. New York, by the Rev. John Abeel, December 5th 1797, Cornelia, daughter of Abraham Lott, formerly Treasurer of the Colony; born November 5th 1761; died New York April 6th 1856; interred alongside of her husband; intestate.

Issue.

1. **Henry Sands,** born March 12th 1770; died young.
2. **Joseph Sands,** born New York, January 7th 1772; died September 2d 1825; left issue male.
3. **Cornelia Sands,** born New York, November 8th 1773; married June 3d 1797 Nathaniel Prime of N. Y.; died N. Y. April 21st 1852.

---

* Comfort Sands and his second wife were originally interred in a plot given to the town of Hoboken by the Stevens family; in 1867 the remains and the gravestones were removed to where they are now. See appendix, page 15.

† For account of the Dodge family see page 73.

‡ Her pall-bearers were: Wm. Seton, J. C. Shaw, Robert Lenox, Henry Cruger, Anthony L. Bleecker, Isaac Roosevelt, Wm. Maxwell, and Wm. Constable.

§ The remains of Comfort Sands' first wife, as also all the remains deposited in his vault in Nassau street were removed 1845 to St. Paul's Church, Eastchester, Westchester Co., N. Y. and placed in a vault, which was closed with the stone taken from the vault in Nassau street. See Appendix, p. 16.

4. **Henry Sands,** born September 8th 1775; died unmarried, May 10th 1817.

5. **Frances Sands,** born November 8th 1776; died unmarried.

6. **Charles Sands,*** born August 26th 1778; died at Lorèze, Languedoc, France, May 15th 1797; interred there; never married.

7. **Louis Sands,** born January 10th 1780; died unmarried July 30th 1809.

8. **Elizabeth Sands,** born June 19th 1781; died young; interred in St. Peter's Church, Philadelphia.

9. **Francis Sands,** born June 3d 1782; died in Hamburg, Germany, November 14th 1799.

10. **Richardson Sands,** born October 24th 1783; died young.

11. **Sidney Sands,** born July 3d 1785; died young.

12. **Augustus Sands,** born May 22d 1786; died June 13th 1805.

13. **Harriet Sands,** born August 17th 1787; died young.

14. **Sarah Maria Sands,** born December 28th 1788; died February 1st 1803.

15. **Frederick William Sands,** born December 5th 1790; died young.

16. **Robert C. Sands,** born May 11th 1799; died unmarried December 16th 1832.

17. **Gertrude Sands,** born August 17th 1801; died young.

18. **Julia Maria Sands,** born March 31st 1805.

Account of Comfort Sands.†

He was named after Comfort Starr, who lived in Danbury, Conn., and who was on a visit to the family soon after his birth; he had a good school education, and at the age of twelve years served as clerk to Stephen Thorne, a

---

* A portrait of him in colored chalk, is in the possession of Rufus Prime's family.

† Written by him and taken from his manuscript book; for account of same, see page 15.

business man on Cowneck, until May 1762, when he went
as clerk to his brother Cornwell Sands in New York and
remained with him one year; from that time he served as a
clerk to Joseph Drake, who kept a store in Peck Slip,
where he lived until May 1769 ; he then opened a store on the
corner of Peck Slip and Queen (now Pearl) Street. He
continued in business and had acquired a large fortune
when the Revolution broke out. In 1776 he purchased a
small farm at New Rochelle to which he removed and
commenced the erection of a spacious house, but before it
was completed, the British landed in October within two
miles of him, and so rapid was their progress, that it was
with difficulty he got his family away, leaving his furniture
and books behind, which were dispersed and his house was
pulled down and the materials all removed to New York
and sold; that same month he went to Philadelphia, but in
consequence of the fear of an attack by the English he
moved in December to a place called the Swamp, about
forty miles distant; in May 1777 he went to Rochester,
N. Y., where he remained until the spring of 1778; he then
went to Schawangunk and in the month of November to
Poughkeepsie, where he staid until April 1780; he then
moved to a farm in the Nine Partners which he occupied
until April 1781; he then again moved to Philadelphia,
which he made his home until June 1783, when, peace being
declared, he went to New Rochelle and from there in October to New York.

From the commencement of the Revolution he was almost
the whole time in the public service.

In July 1783 he formed a partnership with his brother
Joshua Sands and carried on a large business in New York
until 1794.

In 1793 he purchased a lot on Pine Street running
through to Cedar Street, and in 1794 he commenced the
erection of a house thereon, planned by his wife, but before
it was finished, she was taken ill, and after a few days' ill-
ness died.

JAMES I SANDS.
† 1695.

John I Sands. † 1712.
  Edward Sands. † 1769. no issue male.
  Samuel Sands. † 1730. left issue male.
  James II Sands. † 1731. left issue male.
  2 das.

John II Sands. † 1763.
  Nathaniel Sands. † 1750. line extinct.
  Edward Sands. † 1746. left issue male.
  George Sands. † s. p. 4 das.

John III Sands. † 1760. † s. p.
  Robert Sands. † s. p.
  Edward Sands. Ancestor of all the Sands now on Block Isl'd.
  George Sands. † s. p.
  Nath'l Sands. † 1783. left issue male.
  Joshua Sands. † 1787. left issue male.
  Simon Sands. † 1782. left issue male.
  Gideon Sands. † 1776. left issue male.
  Benjamin Sands. † 1824. left issue male. 3 das.

John IV Sands. † 1811. left issue male.
  Cornwell Sands. † 1593. no issue male.
  Elizabeth Sands. † young.
  Robert Sands. † 1825. no issue male.
  Comfort Sands. † 1834.
  Stephen Sands. † 1787. left issue male.
  Richardson Sands. † left issue male.
  Joshua Sands. † 1857. left issue male.
  Joseph Sands. † 1825. left issue male.
  Cornelia Sands. † 1832. = Nath'l Prime.
  Robert C. Sands. † 1832. s. p.
  Julia M. Sands. b. 1805.
  14 children. † s. p.

Appendix.

Memorandum of the several appointments Comfort Sands received
from the State of New York, and other incidents of his life,
from the year 1765. (FROM HIS MANUSCRIPT BOOK AND
OTHER SOURCES.)

1765 assisted in burning ten bales of stamped paper
brought over from London in a brig lying in Burling
Slip, from which vessel they were taken out in the night,
carried to a beach near Colonel Rutgers, where they were
burned.

1769 joined the association not to import goods from
Great Britain until the Tea Act and the Act imposing
duties on glass and paint were repealed.

1774 November, appointed by Congress a member of the
Committee of 60 to carry out their non-importation resolu-
tions.

1775 May, chosen one of the Committee of 100 to carry
further measures into execution, after the battle of Lexing-
ton. November 7th elected one of the 21 members in the
Provincial Congress and served until the 30th of June 1776
and served in that time as one of the Pay Table and also
one of the Committee of Safety.

1776 January, he was directed by the Committee of
Safety, to load three vessels for the West Indies to procure
medicine, powder, and arms, all of which were taken by the
British, also a vessel of his own coming from the West
Indies was carried into Jamaica,— the first vessel taken by
them; she was condemned, vessel and cargo worth $10,000,
and the cost of the condemnation £350, Jamaica currency.
July 24, he was unanimously appointed Auditor General of
the State and served in that Department until he resigned
March 1782.

1777 January, he was appointed one of the Commissioners
to meet at New Haven by order of Congress to regulate the
price of articles for the army.

1778 Member of the Legislature of New York.

1784–1798 Director of the Bank of New York. *
1793–1794 Vice-President of the Chamber of Commerce.
1794–1798 President of the Chamber of Commerce.

Sands Grave Plot.

The Sands plot in the Hoboken Cemetery at New Durham, contains upright gravestones to Comfort Sands, to his second wife and to two of her sisters, also a small obelisk to his son Robert C. Sands, erected by friends of the deceased.

Comfort Sands' Manuscript Book.

This book, containing his notes on the Sands and allied families, and also miscellaneous matters, was left by him to his daughter Julia M. Sands, in whose possession it is at the present time.

Comfort Sands' Family Bible.

His family Bible contains entries by him relating to his first marriage and his children by the same; given by him to his daughter Cornelia Prime; it is now in the possession of the family of Rufus Prime.

Comfort Sands' Residences.

1794 }
1795 } 63 Congress Street, N. Y.

1796, Warehouse, 6 Depeyster Street, residence 26 Pine Street, N. Y.

---

* The first bank established in New York; an original director; he subscribed for 4 shares.

1798 ⎱
1799 ⎰ Warehouse, 13 Cedar Street.

1811 Brooklyn.

1815–1820, 96 Hester Street, N. Y.

1821–1822, 94 Leonard Street, N. Y.

1825 moved to Hoboken, N. J., where he remained until his death in 1834; his widow and daughter Julia M. Sands removed to New York in the autumn of 1834.

Names of persons deposited in the vault of Comfort Sands in the graveyard of the Middle Dutch Church, Nassau Street, between Cedar and Liberty Streets, New York. (FROM COMFORT SANDS' MANUSCRIPT BOOK.)

1788. Harriet, daughter of Comfort Sands.

1788. Henry, son of Comfort Sands; removed from J. Sears' vault.

1788. Sidney, son of Comfort Sands; removed from J. Sears' vault.

1791. Frederick, son of Comfort Sands.

1793. Mr. Delessert, * a friend of his from Paris, France.

1795. Sarah, wife of Comfort Sands.

1796. Mary Dodge, mother of Mrs. Comfort Sands.

1801. Gertrude, a daughter of Comfort Sands.

1802. An infant of Joseph Sands, 14 days old, born May 3d 1802.

1803. Sarah Maria, a daughter of Comfort Sands.

1803. Joseph McPherson, a friend of Comfort Sands.

1804. Emily Frances, a daughter of Nathaniel Prime.

1805. Augustus, a son of Comfort Sands.

1813. Mary Willard, daughter of the Rev. Mr. Willard.

1817. Henry, son of Comfort Sands.

---

* Probably a member of the family of the well-known banker of that name in Paris.

Letters relating to the removal of the Sands remains from Nassau Street to St. Paul's Church, Eastchester, Westchester Co., N. Y.

EDGEWOOD (PELHAM), October 20th 1874.

To RUFUS PRIME, Esq., Huntington, L. I.

I am not certain as to the year the remains were removed from our grandfather's vault in New York to Eastchester, but it was either in 1844 or 1845 * . . .   I find the deed for the vault was given by the Rector of St. Paul's Church, Eastchester, grant to Cornelia Prime; this vault, in which she caused to be placed the remains removed from the vault of her father Comfort Sands, in the Dutch Church in Nassau Street, New York, has no steps or door, but is divided into two parts and covered with heavy marble flags. The division nearest the church contains the remains, the other division was not used. The deed is dated ninth of June 1846, the six being written over five erased, but as it is difficult to get instruments signed properly in country church bodies, it is probable it was prepared for 1845, but not executed until next year.

Your brother,

FREDERICK PRIME.

EDGEWOOD (PELHAM), October 20th, /74.

RUFUS PRIME, Esq.:

Since writing enclosed I find the memorandums respecting an inscription proposed to be placed over the vault containing the remains from Comfort Sands' vault, of which we talked last year. In one of yours you seem to think the vault was under the Church; this is a mistake; it is very near but on the outside of the south-east wall of the church. I will put a rough diagram on the back of this.

Your affectionate brother,

FREDERICK PRIME.

---

* It was in 1845; Rufus Prime assisted at this removal, he was in Europe in 1844, but was in New York during the spring of 1845.

2

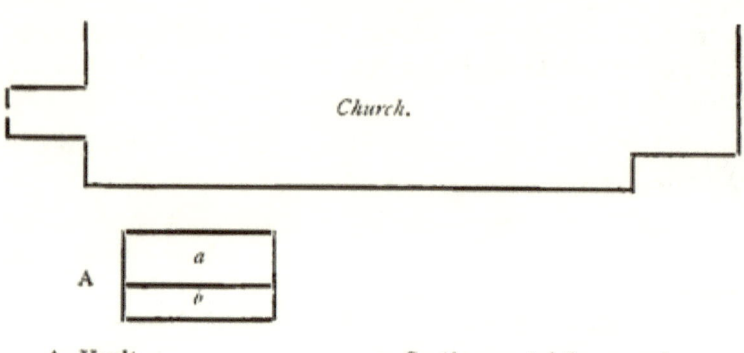

A. Vault.   a. Section containing remains.
                          b. Section not used.

The vault was a square solid wall of masonry, divided by a cross-wall, making as it were two distinct pits; as I was entirely ignorant of what space would be required, when the remains came, one division was found to be twice as large as was necessary — the covering flags were long, rough, and heavy, each flag long enough, I think, to extend over both divisions from side to side.*

Names of persons interred in the Sands Burying-ground on Cowneck, L. I., given by John I Sands. (FROM COMFORT SANDS' MANUSCRIPT BOOK.)

George Sands, son of John I, died young.
John I Sands, March 15th, 1712.
Sybil, wife of John I Sands, December 23d, 1733.
John II Sands, August 30th, 1763.
Catherine, wife of John II Sands, February 10th, 1769.
John III Sands, November 22d, 1760.
Elizabeth, wife of John III Sands, May 10th, 1793.

---

* The gravestone which was over the vault in Nassau Street is now over this one.

Robert Sands, son of John II, April 12th, 1735 25
Gideon Sands, son of John II, April 20th, 1770 41
Henry Sands, son of Edward II, July 1st, 1781 54
Martha Sands, his wife, daughter of Samuel Cornell,
    November 28th, 1759 31
Richard Sands, son of Edward II, October 26th, 1798 . 69
Deborah Sands, his wife, daughter of —— Griffin,
    March 16th, 1799 69
Mary, wife of Benjamin Sands, November 16th, 1798 . 59
George Sands, son of John II, January 15th, 1777 . . . 60
Dorothy Bowne, daughter of John I Sands, 1765 . . . 62
Edward Sands, son of John I, March 9th, 1746 55
Ray Sands, son of Edward II, February 14th, 1739.
Mary, daughter of Richard and Deborah Sands, 1753.
Sybil Thorne, daughter of Edward Sands, March 1st, 1759 32
Mary Sands, daughter of John II, March 15th, 1724 . . 9
Mary Guilford, daughter of John II, February 19th, 1755 23
Elizabeth, daughter of Simon and Catherine Sands,
    June 17th, 1752.
Elizabeth Sands, daughter of John III, September 13th,
    1747 6
Jerusha, daughter of Benjamin and Mary Sands, wife
    of William Sands, April 14th, 1795 28
Mary, daughter of Gideon and Mary Sands, August 1st,
    1778 15
Simon Sands, son of John II, April 5th, 1782 55
Catherine, first wife of Simon Sands, December 28th, 1764 33
William Sutton, second husband to Mary, widow of
    Gideon Sands, August 13th, 1780 45
Thomas Thorne, husband of Abigail, daughter of
    Henry Sands, May 15th, 1797 44
Abigail Thorne, daughter of Henry and Martha Sands 44
Mary Sutton, wife of William Sutton, July 28th, 1793 . 60
Henry Sands, son of Richard and Deborah Sands,
    January 1st, 1798 38
Hannah, daughter of Henry and Martha Sands, 1753 . 5
Mary, daughter of Henry and Martha Sands, 1768 . . 17

Deborah Mott, daughter of Edward Sands, second wife
of Edmund Mott, September 1st, 1762 26
Nathaniel Sands, son of John I, 1750 63
John Sands, son of the above Nathaniel, 1764 30
Mary, daughter of Richard Smith, wife of John Sands,
December 21st, 1805 76
Elizabeth Sands, wife of John IV, March 8th, 1806 . . 70
John IV Sands, June 25th, 1811 74
Robert Sands, son of John IV, 1812 41
Edmund Mott, husband of Deborah, 1813 67
Ray Sands, son of Richard and Deborah, 1815 46
Elizabeth, wife of Griffin Sands, 1815 31
George Guthrie Sands, son of Benjamin and Mary, 1812 43
Deborah Sands, daughter of Richard and Deborah, 1816 40
Clarina Sands, daughter of Richard II, 1816.
Treadwell, son of Simon Sands, 1812 45
Hannah, daughter of Joshua and Mary, 1802 38
Twin of Thomas Thorne, 1778, a few days old.
Infant of Thomas Thorne, 1783.
Abigail, wife of Thomas Thorne, 1794 36
Leonard, son of Thomas Thorne, 1795 10
Henry Sands Thorne, son of Thomas Thorne, 1811 . . 30
Simon, son of Nathaniel Marston, 1787 7
Simon, son of Nathaniel Marston, 1791 3
An infant of Nathaniel Marston, 1792.
Anna, daughter of Simon and Catherine Sands, 1778 . 22
Elizabeth, daughter of Simon and Catherine Sands, 1777 23
Sarah, daughter of John and Elizabeth, 1774, young.
Joshua, son of John and Elizabeth, 1778, young.

Farms owned by the Sands family on Cowneck, L. I.

John I Sands, purchased December 25th, 1691, of Richard
Cornell of Rockaway, and of Elizabeth his wife, consideration £200, 500 acres on Cowneck; this land Cornell held
under a grant from Governor Dongan of 1686.

This tract was made up of three parcels:

a. The Home Farm.
b. The Farm occupied by Richard Sands.
c. 100 acres on Sheet's Creek.

A.

The Home Farm, on which is the Sands burying-ground, was occupied and built upon by John I Sands; on his death, 1712, it passed to his second son Nathaniel Sands, who in 1733 sold it to John II Sands, who moved there, made it his home, and died there; on his death, 1763, it fell to his two sons Simon and Benjamin Sands, who about 1765 divided it; the Homestead fell to Benjamin Sands, who sold it to his son-in-law, Benjamin Hewlett; the share of Simon Sands was built upon by him and was eventually also sold to Benjamin Hewlett.

B.

This farm was left by John I Sands to his second son Nathaniel, who sold it to Edward Sands.

C.

This farm was left by John I Sands to his second son Nathaniel Sands, who sold it to William Cornell.

The Inland Farm.

In 1716 John II Sands purchased a farm in the interior of Cowneck; in 1733 it passed to his son John III Sands, who in 1735 built a house * there, in which all his children were born; on his death, 1760, it passed to his son John IV Sands; John III Sands' widow lived there until her death in 1793.

---

* On the road from Sands' Point to Roslyn, there stands on the right hand, on Flower Hill, third house from the School House, a spacious farm-house, the property of E. Willet's family; this is the house in which Comfort Sands, and his brothers and sisters were born.

Letters from Block Island addressed to Comfort Sands in 1808.

(FROM COMFORT SANDS' MANUSCRIPT BOOK.)

NEW SHOREHAM, February 15th day, 1808.

RESPECTED KINSMAN.

I received your note by the hands of Captain Littlefield, and the readiness to comply with your request is what I always had a desire to obtain, as I think it an honor to me that I descended from so ancient, so honorable, so respectable a family as our ancestors were.

James Sands * came from the town of Reading, in Berkshire, England, to Plymouth, in the State of Massachusetts, about the year 1658,† and removed to Block Island about the year 1662, and was one of the sixteen proprietors who purchased the island of the natives, and was largely concerned in settling the township, and was one who petitioned the General Assembly for a charter of Incorporation, which was obtained in the year 1672 by the name of Shoreham. Since which it has been altered to New Shoreham. By which charter we have the privilege of choosing all our officers for the regulating of the police of the town. James * Sands' will was made the 18th June, 1694. James Sands died the 13th day of March, 1695, aged 73 years, leaving four sons, namely, John, Samuel, James, and Edward, and two daughters, Sarah and Mercy. Sarah married to Nathaniel Niles, and Mercy with Joshua Raymond. Sarah Sands, wife of James * Sands' will was made the 17th day of October, 1703, and Edward Sands the son of James * died in the year 1708, leaving one daughter, who married with Teddiman Hull; James Sands'* deed to John Sands‡ is dated the 15th§ day of November, 1690, and

* James I Sands.
† This date is not correct; he was already on this side of the water in 1642.
‡ John I Sands.
§ For "15" read "5."

is recorded* at Hempstead, New Book of Records, in pages 345 and 346 by Thomas Gildersleve, Town Clarke.

John † Sands, son of John ‡ Sands, was born the 22d day of January, 1683; Edward Sands, the son of James § Sands by Mary his wife, had a daughter born the 30th day of January, 1703–4, named Sarah Sands; and from the removal of John ‡ Sands, Samuel Sands, and James Sands to Cowneck, Long Island, which must have been about the year 1691 or 1692, until John † Sands, son of John ‡ Sands, and grandson of James, § returned and married ‖ with Catherine Guthrie, daughter of Robert Guthrie, which was in the year 1706.

John ¶ Sands, son of John † Sands, and Catherine his wife was born the 1 day of January 1708.

Robert Sands, the son of John Sands † and Catherine his wife was born the 26 day of December 1710.

Edward Sands, the son of John † Sands, and Catherine his wife was born the 16 day of March 1719.**

And from the removal of John † Sands, our grandfather, to Cowneck there appears to be a length of time I can find no account of our family until my father's marriage with Hannah Tredwell, daughter of Benjamin Tredwell of Great Neck, which must have been about the year 1734, who had children born.

---

* Reference to records not correct; the deed is recorded at Jamaica, North Hempstead Town Records, Liber 2, fol. 70.

† John II Sands.

‡ John I Sands.

§ James I Sands.

‖ "Rhode Island.

"These may certify whom it may concern that Captain John Sands and Catherine Guthrie, both of Shoreham, al'as Block Island, were on the 9th day of September, in the year one thousand seven hundred and six, at Newport, joined together in the honorable estate of matrimony, by Samuel Cranston, Governor."

¶ John III Sands.

** Not correct; Edward was born January 17th 1712, his sister Anne was born March 16th 1719.

Ray Sands, son of Edward Sands and Hannah his wife, was born the 18 day of June 1739.

Peggy Sands, daughter of Edward Sands and Hannah his wife, was born the 18 day of July 1742.

John Sands, son of Edward Sands and Hannah his wife, was born the 13 day of August 1745.

Edward Sands, son of Edward Sands and Hannah his wife, was born the 13 day of April 1748.

Hannah Sands, wife of Edward Sands, died the 18 day of January 1760, in the 51 year of her age.

Captain Edward Sands, married to Lucy Clarke, the 15 day of September 1763 at South Kingston.

Captain Edward Sands departed this life on the 21 day October of 1778, in the 67th year of his age.

Edward Sands, son of Edward Sands, was married to Deborah Niles, the 14 day of December 1769, and had a daughter born the 23 day of November 1770, named Anna Sands; and had a son born the 28 day of August 1774, named William Pitt Sands, and had a daughter born the 1 day of January 1779, named Hannah Tredwell Sands.

Ray Sands, the son of Edward Sands and Hannah his wife; died the 1 day of February 1808, in the 71 year of his age.

N. B. We have it from tradition that James * Sands was married before he left England, and that his wife's maiden name was Sarah Walker, and that he brought some of his children out with him when he came to Plymouth.

Thus you see, my kinsman, I have given you as particular an account of our family as the nature and circumstances will admit of. Unless I descend into my brothers' and sister's family, which you may think noways material in your inquiry, and you will find that I now stand Edward Sands, which was the son of Edward, which was the son of John, which was the son of James,† who came from

---

* James I Sands.

† This is not correct : he has omitted one John.

the town of Reading, in Berkshire, England, and remain with every sentiment of respect, dear sir, your humble servant,

EDWARD SANDS.

NEW SHOREHAM, February 28th 1808.

DEAR SIR:

In answer to a letter which I received from you some time past respecting our family, I have taken all the pains in my power to obtain all the information that can be obtained, both here and at Rhode Island, as respects James * Sands; can't find what time he came from England. I have been informed by my father in his lifetime, and he had his information from his uncle Simon † Ray, who well remembered James Sands, that he, James Sands, came from the town of Reading, county of Berkshire, in England, and that he first landed at Plymouth in Boston State. I find by the first settlement of Block Island, that in the year 1660, he, the said James Sands with a number of others sent a man and purchased Block Island of the natives, and in April 1661 they embarked from Taunton in the Bay State and came to Block Island and settled the same, and divided it into sixteen shares, and he owned one-sixteenth. I find by his last will made and executed on the 18th day of June, 1694, that he had six children, namely, John ‡ the eldest, James, Samuel, and Edward, and two daughters, Sarah and Mercy, and in March 1695, he died aged 73 years, as appears by his gravestone. To his son John ‡ he gave lands by deed, to his other sons by will. As respects his marriage can give no information, but that his wife's name was Sarah as mentioned in his will, nor what her name was before marriage; but am of opinion he married before he came out from England; as to the death of his wife, can't find any account, no stone to be found or record, but that she outlived him as by will, he had no brother, he was the only one of the name;

---

* James I Sands.　　　† Simon III Ray.　　　‡ John I Sands.

it is a mistake as respects his brother; it was his youngest*
son Edward who is buried by his side; as appears by his
gravestone the time of his death was 1708, and his age, can't
tell, but that he left one child, a daughter, which daughter
married with a Hull, which there is not a very large family
descended from.

John † Sands, son of James, ‡ as it appears by your letter
that you have found who he married with, which is correct.
James and Samuel, I can find no account of their marriage,
nor who with, nor when they moved from Block Island. I
find from the records of the town, that they sold their lands
soon after the death of their father. I judge from that cir-
cumstance, that they left here about 1696 or 1697; by the
enclosed certificate § you will find the names of the persons
his two daughters married with, which is all the information I am able to give respecting them. As to time of their
death, and number of children, I can give no information,
only that there is a large family descended from them, and
that their families are scattered in the New England
States.

At what time our grandfather ‖ removed from here I find
no account, but you may judge from the age of his three
oldest children, which were born here. Myself should sup-
pose it was 1713.

As respects the old paternal estate of James ‡ Sands, I
own his first purchase, and part of Robert Guthrie's, which
was the land he gave to his son John † by deed. The homestead where he lived and died, he gave to his son Edward, is

---

* For "youngest" read "second."

† John I Sands.

‡ James I Sands.

§ "Nathaniel Niles and Sarah Sands, daughter of James Sands, were
married February 14th 1671. Joshua Raymond was married to
Mercy Sands, daughter of James Sands the 29 day of April 1683, and
in the year 1704 the said Joshua Raymond died, and sometime after
his widow and children moved to New London, North Parish, in the
State of Connecticut."

‖ John II Sands.

in the Hull family, which I fear wont remain long. The enclosed certificates * will give you all the information I can get from the town records; should there be any further information in my power to obtain for you, I would do it with pleasure, and am with great respect your affectionate kinsman, JOHN SANDS.

Letter in the matter of a presumed Portrait of Comfort Sands.

NEW YORK, December 8th, 1879.
156 East 37th Street.

RUFUS PRIME, Esq., 147 West 14th St., N. Y.

My Dear Rufus: In answer to your inquiries as to whether there exists a portrait of my father, your grandfather, Mr. Comfort Sands, I have to say that I have never heard of the existence of one.

In this connection I send you an abstract from a letter on this subject, addressed to me by my niece, your cousin, Mrs. Mary Sands Griffin, written in Dresden, Germany, on the 11th of February, 1879:

---

* "Robert Gutterege and Margaret Williams *(a)* widow were married June 5 1689, and Catherine Gutterege their daughter was born the 24 day of June 1690, and the above said Robert Gutterege died December the 3d 1692.

"John Sands, *(b)* the son of John *(c)* Sands, and Catherine his wife, was born on the first day of January 1708.

"Robert Sands, the son of John *(c)* Sands, and Catherine his wife, was born on the 26 day of December 1710.

"Edward Sands, the son of John *(c)* Sands, and Catherine his wife, was born on the 17 day of January 1711–12.

"Sarah Sands, daughter of Edward and Mary Sands, was born January 30th 1693–4.

Witness: WALTER RATHBUN, *Town Clk.*"

---

a for "Margaret," read "Anna." Verified by me from the Record Book on Block Island.

b John III Sands.

c John II Sands.

"You ask me about a portrait of your father, my grandfather. I never had nor even saw one. The likeness Arthur Sands has, was of my father Joseph Sands, taken in Paris about 1800. I gave it to Louis Sands, who I believe, left it in Arthur's charge. It is in a heavy antique frame."

Very truly yours,

JULIA M. SANDS.

Extracts from Niles's [*] Narrative. (PUBLISHED: MASSA-CHUSETTS HIST. SOC. 3D SER. VI.)

At Block Island, where I was born, some time after the Island began to be settled by the English, there then being but sixteen Englishmen and a boy, and about three hundred Indians, the Indians were wont, some of them, to treat the English in a surly, lordly manner, which moved the English to suspect they had some evil designs in hand; and it being in the time of Philip's war, there was a large stone house garrisoned, erected by James [†] Sands, Esq., one of the first settlers. . . . The before mentioned James Sands, who was the leading man among them, entered into a wigwam, where he saw a very fine brass gun standing, and an Indian fellow lying on a bench in the wigwam, probably to guard and keep it. Mr. Sands' curiosity led him to take and view it, as it made a curious and uncommon appearance. Upon which the Indian fellow rises up hastily and snatches the gun out of his hand, and withal gave such a violent thrust with the butt end of it as occasioned him to stagger backward. But feeling something under his feet, he espied it to be a hoe, which he took up and improved, and with it fell upon the Indian. Upon which a mighty scuffle ensued, the English and Indians on the outside of the wigwam closing in one with another; which probably would have issued in the destruction of the whole English

---

[*] He was a son of Nathaniel Niles and of Sarah Sands, a daughter of James I Sands.

[†] James I Sands.

party. . . . Mrs. Hutchinson, who came into this country
under a religious character, probably not very long after
the church at Boston was settled. . . . went farther
westward to a place called Eastchester, now in the eastern
part of the province of New York. . . . In order to
pursue her purpose, she agreed with the before-mentioned
Captain James* Sands, then a young man, to build her
house, and he took a partner with him in the business.
When they had near spent their provisions, he sent his
partner for meat, which was to be fetched at a considerable
distance. While his partner was gone, there came a company of Indians to the frame where he was at work, and
made a great shout and sat down. After some time they
gathered up his tools, put his broad-axe on his shoulder,
and his other tools into his hands, and made signs to him
to go away. But he seemed to take no notice of them, but
continued in his work. At length one of them said, " Ye-
hah Mumune Ketok," the English of which is, " Come, let
us go," and they all went away to the waterside for clams
or oysters. After some time they came back, and found
him still at work as before. They again gathered up his
tools, put them into his hands as before they had done,
with the like signs moving him to go away. He still seemed
to take no notice of them, but kept on in his business, and
when they had stayed some time they said as before, " Ye-
hah Mumune Ketok." Accordingly they all went away,
and left him there at his work, a remarkable instance of
the restraining power of God on the hearts of these furious
and merciless infidels, who otherwise would doubtless, in
their rage, have split his brains with his own axe. But
God had further business for him to do in this world, in
conducting the affairs on Block Island afterwards, as
before is briefly related, for many years when the people
there became more numerous, and until his eldest son,
Captain John † Sands, a gentleman of great port and superior
powers succeeded him. He died in the 72d year of his age.

---

* James I Sands.   † John I Sands.

He was a benefactor to the poor; for as his house was garrisoned, in the time of their fear of the Indians, as before is noted, many poor people resorted to it, and were supported mostly from his liberality. He was also a promoter of religion in his benefactions to the minister they had there in his day, though not altogether so agreeable to him as might be desired, as being inclined to the Anabaptist persuasion. He devoted his house for the worship of God, where it was attended every Lord's day or Sabbath.

His wife was a gentlewoman of remarkable sobriety and piety, given also to hospitality. She was the only midwife and doctress on the island, or rather a doctor, all her days, with very little, and with some, and mostly, no reward at all. Her skill in surgery was doubtless very great, from some instances I remember she told me of.

Mr. Sands had a plentiful estate, and gave free entertainment to all gentlemen who came to the island; and when his house was garrisoned it became an hospital, for several poor people resorted thither, as before is remarked, who being driven from their habitations and improvements, could bring but little with them. I heard his wife (who outlived her husband many years) often with admiration express the singular tokens of God's favorable providence in that time, by increasing remarkably the comforts of life on themselves and the poor that Providence had cast under their care.

I shall give but one remarkable instance more in this digression, with relation to Mrs. Sands, of whom I have been speaking. She had then but one little child, a girl, just able to run about and prattle a little. Her maid had occasion to go into the field on some business, and urged that the child might go with her. The mistress denied, and withal telling the maid there was an old well in the field, which the child would be likely to fall into, or some other mischief would happen to her. The maid goes away, and the mother sits down in the doorway, to keep the child out of danger, as they had a mill-pond near the house; and as sewing linen cloth, and wanted a piece that lay on the

table on the opposite part of the room, she bid the child
bring it to her. The child went to a door that led into an
inner room, where there was no other passage out, and
closing the door, saying, "This, mamma, this?" she said,
"No, that," pointing to the cloth. She was busy and thought
no more of her child, until one of her neighbors came and
said, "The Lord give you patience; your child is drowned."
The man came by the child, and saw it floating on the
water in the flume, but took no care of it, but went up to
the house — whereas if he had taken it out, he might have
been a means of preserving its life. But thus it must be in
Providence. The mother often lamented her presumption,
in pretending to be her child's keeper. . . .

It is time to return to Mr. Sands, where we left him,
working on his frame . . . the Indians being gone, he
gathered up his tools, and drew off, and in his way met his
partner bringing provisions, to whom he declared the nar-
row escape he had made for his life. Resolving not to
return, and run a further risk of the like kind, they both
went from the business . . .

Captain James Sands . . . had four sons, all living on
Block Island, until the island was infested, and plundered
twice by French privateers; after which the three elder
brothers removed to Long Island, and settled there (from
whom I had the narrative of what I am now writing),
namely Captain John * Sands, Mr. James and Samuel Sands,
each of them leaving a farm at Block Island, which they
stocked with sheep, and were wont to come once a year at
their shearing time on the island, to carry off their wool
and what fat sheep there were at that time, and market at
New York. Upon this design they were all coming together,
sometime in the beginning of June, and as near as I can
remember, in the year 1702, one of them bringing a little
daughter, about seven years of age, in a new vessel he had
built, designing to leave the child with his mother for some
time, Mrs. Sarah Sands, the famous doctor I spake of

---

* John I Sands.

before, who was then living a widow; and several Indian
servants were in the forecastle or fore part of the vessel,
which was enclosed, but there was no bulk-head abaft,
where these gentlemen were sitting together. There was
also a quantity of wheat in the hold under the deck, which
lay partly at the lower part of the mast. As they were
sailing down the Sound, as it is called, between Long Island
and the mainland, under an easy, pleasant gale of wind, they
observed a dark, threatening cloud gathering in the north-
west. Apprehending a sudden gust of wind, they pulled
down their sails, as they saw at a distance also a rippling of
the water,— and it proved accordingly. But the cloud
scattered, and the gust went over, and they hoisted their
sails and proceeded in their course as before. After a short
time the cloud gathered again, and being apprehensive of a
like sudden gust, they lowered their sails; and it proved as
they expected, and they again proceeded on their voyage
with a fair and easy gale. But in a space of time the
cloud gathered a third time, and appeared more terrible,
threatening an extraordinary tempest; upon which they
lowered their sails, as they had twice before. And it proved
very terrible, with thunder, lightning, rain and wind, with
stress and uncommon violence. At length there came a
loud clap of thunder with sharp lightning, and struck on
the top of their mast; and the lightning ran down into the
hold of the vessel to the step of the mast, and then suddenly
started upward; and they saw apparently the wheat that lay
near the mast fly each way from it, and seemed to disperse;
but it soon gathered into a round solid body, as big, or big-
ger, than a man's fist, and in that form flew to one side of
the vessel, and then broke with an extraordinary loud noise
as of hard thunder, and then seemed to scatter; but then
gathered into the like form as before, and flew to the other
side of the vessel, and broke with the like mighty noise,
and dispersed; but gathered the third time, and flew back to
the other side, where it made a hole between wind and
water, and disappeared. The child, before mentioned, lay
all this time asleep, while the lightning passed forward and

backward over it, as has been related, without the least
hurt, when her father, and uncles with him, that beheld the
lightning in its motions and operations, as plainly as to see
from one side of the room to the other, concluded she was
struck dead as she lay. Nor were any hurt in the vessel,
except these men's eyes were so sore they scarcely could see
when they came to the island,— where I then was, and from
them received the narrative, as here is related, of this won-
derful salvation God wrought for them.   .   .   .

Sometime in July, 1689, three French privateer vessels
came to Block Island.   .   .   .   As they were thus become
masters of the island, they disarmed the men, and stove their
guns to pieces on the rocks, and carried the people and con-
fined them in the house of Captain James* Sands before
mentioned, which was large and accommodable for their
purpose, and not far from the harbor. This they made
their prison.   .   .   .   The French came a third time while
I was on the island, and came to anchor on Saturday,
sometime before night; and acquainted us who they were
and what they intended, by hoisting up their white colors.
None of the people appearing to oppose them, and having
at this time my aged grandparents, Mr. James* Sands and
his wife, before mentioned, to take care of, with whom I
then dwelt; knowing also that if they landed they would
make his house the chief seat of their rendezvous, as they
had done twice before, and not knowing what insults or
outrage they might commit on them, I advised to the leaving their house, and betaking themselves to the woods for
shelter, till they might return under prospects of safety,
which they consented to. Accordingly we took our flight
into the woods, which were at a considerable distance,
where we encamped that night as well as the place and
circumstances would allow, with some others, that for the
like reasons fell into our company.

---

* James I Sands.

Will of John II Sands. (SURROGATE'S OFFICE, N. Y., LIBER 24, FOL. 224.)

In the Name of God Amen this twentyeth seventh day of February Anno Domini Seventeen hundred fifty and nine I John Sands of the Township of Heampstead in Queens County and in the Province of New York Yeoman being in Bodily health and of perfect mind and memory do make and ordain and constitute this my last Will and Testament.

Imprimis. I Will impower and authorize my Executors hereafter named in some Convenient time after my Decease in their Discretion to sell and convey all my land which I have at Block Island my son Edward Sands to have the first refusal and in case my son Edward should refuse to give the full value of the aforesaid land I then order my Executors to make sale of the aforesaid land by way of publick vendue or otherwise as my Executors shall think proper and out . . the money arising from the sales above said I will my funerill Expenses and just debts and Legacies hereafter mentioned and bequeathed be paid and discharged & if in case there should be any money over and above arising from the above sales then will pay all my debts and Legacies, then my Will is that my son Benjamin Sands shall have the remainder.

Item. I give and bequeath unto my five sons John Sands Edward Sands Nathaniel Sands Joshua Sands & Gideon Sands to each and every one of them the sum of five Shillings Current Lawfull money of New York.

Item. I give and bequeath unto my Daughter Anne Brooks what goods she hath in her possession of mine and my negro Girl Moll and five shillings Current Lawfull money of New York.

Item. I give unto my Grandson Dean twenty pounds Current Lawfull money of New York the above said Legacies to be paid in some convenient time after the above said land is sold.

Item. I give bequeath and devise unto my true and loving Wife Catherine Sands in Lieu of her right of dowery the use profit and advantages of the one third part of my farm that I now dwell on during her natural life and the one equal half of my buildings on the same during her Widowhood and no longer and all my household goods within dores at her own disposal (Except my Silver Tankard & Clock) I give bequeath unto my Wife my Slave named Herciles and my two negro Woman named Pegg and her Daughter Isabell and the one equal third part of my farming utencills and the one third part of my sheep and hogs and three good Cows and a young Mare Nobby at her own disposall.

Item. I give and bequeath unto the family of the Sandses for ever for a burying place a piece of land six Rods square in my Orchard round the burying place that is thereon Cowneck and on the farm that I now live on.

Item. I give and bequeath unto my two sons George and Simon Sands all that farm of mine lying and being on the bottom of Cowneck with the Creeks meadows thereunto belonging except four acres of land to my son Simon Sands his heirs and assigns for ever to be taken out of the farm and then the remainder part of my above said farm to them their heirs and assigns for ever (under these following conditions with all the building and improvements equally to be divided in quantity and quality and nevertheless that if in case my Son George Sands should Dye without Lawfull Issue then I give and devise that part of my Real Estate bequeathed to him to be equally divided between my three sons Simon Gideon and Benjamin Sands to them their heirs and assigns for ever.

Item. I give and bequeath unto my son Simeon Sands my Clock.

Item. I give and bequeath unto my Son Benjamin Sands my Silver Tankard.

Item. the Remainder part of my farming utensills Cattles Horses hoggs and Sheep to be equally between my two Sons George and Simeon Sands.

Item. I give and bequeath unto my Son George Sands my young negro man named Mical and I hereby appoint ordain and constitute my Wife Catherine Sands and my two sons Simeon Sands and Gideon Sands and my kinsman Henry Sands all of the Township of Hempstead and in the Province of New York to be my whole and Sole Executrix and Executors of this my last Will and Testament and I do hereby give them my whole Strength power and authority to act in the premises before mentioned and I do hereby revoke and disanull all and every other former Will Testament Legacy and bequeathment Executors and Executrix by me before this time made Willed given bequeathed nominated and named and I do confirm this and no other to be last will and Testament whereof and for further confirmation I have hereunto set my hand and affixed my seal the day and year first above written.

JOHN SANDS (L. S.)

Signed Sealed Published Pronounced and Declared by the said John Sands to be his last Will and Testament in the presents of uss John Cornwall, William Cornwall, Joshua Cornwall.

Will of John III Sands. (SURROGATE'S OFFICE, N. Y., LIBER 22, FOL. 363.)

In the name of God Amen this ninth day of October in the year of our Lord Christ Ano que Domina one thousand seven hundred & Sixty I John Sands Junr. of Cowneck in the Township of Hamsted in Queens County & in the Province of New York Yeoman Being in perfect mind and of sound memory thanks be given unto God & calling unto mind the mortality of my body & knowing thats appointed for all men once to Dye do make & ordain this my last Will & Testament that is to say Principally & first of all I give & Recommend my soul into the hands of Almighty God that gave it & my Body I Recommend to the Earth to

be buried in decent Christian Burial at the Discretion of
my Executors hereafter named nothing doubting but at
the generall Resurrection I shall Receive the same again by
the mighty Power of God and as touching such Worldly
Estate as it Hath Pleased God to bless me with in this Life
I give Devise & dispose of the same in the following manner and form Imprimis I Will that my true & loveing Wife
Elizabeth Sands shall Pay Interest for all the mony my
Estate shall be indebted for at my Decease untill my loveing Son Robert Sands shall arrive to ye age of twenty one
years. Item. I give and bequeath unto my true & loveing
Wife Elizabeth Sands all my houshold goods & furniture &
one negro Girl called by name Sarah & one negro man
called by name Warrick with all the Plate belonging or
appertaining unto me to her her heirs & assigns for ever in
Lieu of her Dowry and the use of all my farm I now Live
on with the rights and Priviledges of ye Creeks at the
Bottom of Cow Neck & all the Stock and farming utensills
appertaining or belonging thereunto for the bringing up
my children in a decent Christian manner untill my said
son Robert Sands shall arrive to the years of twenty one
If she remains my widow but if she should either Dye or or
marry within the term of time above said I then order my
Executors to Rent out my said Farm & the money arising
therefrom to go towards bringing up my said Children I
also order my Executors hereafter named that whom soever
shall Rent the said Farm shall not cut nor destroy any
more Timber & Firewood than shall be really necessary for
the use of such a farm and my said Wife Elizabeth Sands
is to deliver up with the Farm all the Stock and Farming
Utensils in as good Order as when received them as shall
be Judged by my Executors at the coming to age of my
son Robert Sands and when my said son Robert Sands shall
arrive to the years of Twenty one I then order my Executors to vallue all my whole Farm with the Salt meadows
at the bottom of Cow Neck & all my stock and and Farming
Utensills appertaining or belonging thereunto which I order

my Executors to give my true and loveing Son John Sands
the Refusall thereof which if he should except of ye said
Farm Stock and Utensills all the Valuation of the Executors as abovesaid and the money to be Paid at a Reasonable
time after the valuation of said Farm Stock and utensills and
in case the said John Sands should not except of the said
Farm Stock and Utensills as above said I then order my
Executors to Expose of the said Farm Stock and Utensills
at Publick Sale only Reserving the Dwelling house to my
Dear and loving Wife as long as she Remains my Widow
and the money arising therefrom I give devise and Dispose
of in the manner following after paying my Just debts.
Item I give and bequeath unto my true and loving Son
John Sands the sum of two hundred and fifty pounds to
him his heirs and assigns for ever Item, I give and bequeath unto my loving son Cornwell Sands the sum of two
hundred pounds to be paid by Executors two months after
my Decease also one negro boy called by name Mike and
as much more as shall make equal with the rest of my Sons
hereafter named at the Sale of the Farm to him his heirs
and assigns for ever. Item. I give and bequeath unto my
five youngest Sons all namely Robert Sands Comfort Sands
Stephen Sands Richardson Sands and Joshua Sands all
the remainder of my Estate to be equally Divided between
them at a reasonable time after the Sale of my farm to
them their heirs and assigns for and if either of my said
sons should Dye before they arrive to the age of twenty
one or without Lawfull Issue their Legacies to be equally
divided between the surviving Bretheren and I do likewise
Constitute and appoint my true and loving wife Elizabeth
Sands and my loving Brother George Sands and my true
and trusty Friend Stephen Thorne as my whole and
sole Executors and Executrix and I do hereby utterly
disallow Revok voke and Disannull all and every other
Former Testaments Wills Legacies and bequeaths and
Executors by me in any before named Willed and Bequeath
Rattyfying and confirming this and no other to be my last

Will and Testament,   In Witness whereof I have hereunto
sett my hand and seal the day and year above said

JOHN SANDS, Junr.   (seal).

Signed, Sealed Published and Declared by the said John
Sands Junior as his last Will and Testament in the Presents
of us who are here present.

Rogr Fenonilet.   Elizabeth Mott   William Eixon.

RAY.

SIMON I RAY.

Died: at Braintree, Mass., September 30th 1641.

Will: referred to in Index to Vol. I. of Probate Court of . . . . ; the copy of the Will itself was on one of the lost pages; inventory of February 20th 1642, shows good estate.

Married: 1st. in England . . .

———— 2dly. in America, a widow George.

Issue.

1. **Simon II Ray,** of whom later.
2. **Mary Ray,** married November 15th —— Samuel Deering.

Account of Simon I Ray.

Of Braintree, Mass., came, it is said, from Braintree, co. Essex, England; landed at Plymouth, brought with him his son Simon II Ray, then about six years of age.

SIMON II RAY.

Born : in England 1635.

Died : on Block Island March 17th 1737; buried there.*

Married : 1st. 1661, Mary da. of Nathaniel I Thomas †
of Marshfield.

———— 2dly. —— widow of ——

Will : 1727.

Issue.

1. **Sybil Ray,** born March 19th 1665; married John I
Sands of Cowneck, L. I.

2. **Mary Ray,** born May 19th 1667; married an
Englishman; was the first American woman presented to
the King.

———

* His tomb in the burying-ground on Block Island, of slate, and
recumbent, bears upon it :

> "This monument
> Is erected to the Memory
> Of Simon Ray Esquire,
> One of the original Proprietors
> Of this Island
> He was largely concerned
> In settling the Township,
> And was one of the chief Magistrates.
> And such was his Benevolence,
> That besides the Care which he took
> Of their civil Interests,
> He frequently instructed them,
> In the most important Concerns
> Of our Holy Religion.
> He was deprived of his Eyesight many Years,
> Chearfully submitting to the will of God,
> His life being in this trying Instance,
> As in all others,
> A lovely example of Christian Virtue.
> He died on the 17th of March 1737
> In the 102nd year of his age."

† For account of Thomas family see page 50.

3. **Dorothy Ray,** born October 16th 1669; married —— Clapp, of Rye, N. Y.

4. **Simon III Ray,** of whom later.

5. —— **Ray,** married Samuel Sands, brother of John I Sands.

Account of Simon II Ray.

One of the original settlers on Block Island in 1662.

1671 September, tax-rater on Block Island.

1687 June, Justice present at the Court of Common Pleas at Newport.

1688 Quarter-session Justice.

1705 Deputy from Block Island.

SIMON III RAY.

Born: on Block Island 1670.

Died: on Block Island March 9th 1755; buried there.*

---

* His tomb in the burying-ground on Block Island, of slate, and recumbent, bears upon it the following epitaph:

> "Beneath This Stone
> Are deposited the Remains
> Of Simon Ray Esquire,
> Who for many Years,
> Was one of the chief Magistrates of this Town.
> He filled the most important Offices
> With honor to Himself
> And advantage to his Country.
> To suppress Vice and promote Virtue,
> Was the fixed aim of his private Life,
> And public Authority,
> He was a lover of Learning
> Justice and Benevolence
> A Friend to his Country and attentive
> To the Interests of this Island.

Married: 1st. Judith Mainwaring, of New London, Conn.

———— 2dly. Deborah, daughter of Job Greene, and of his wife Phœbe, of Warwick, R. I.

Issue.

1. **Simon IV Ray,** followed the sea; died before his father; left no issue.

2. **Gideon Ray,** followed the sea; died before his father; left no issue.

3. **Nathaniel Ray,** a farmer; father of Simon V Ray; he and his son both died young, and left no issue living.

4. **Mary Ray,** married 1724 John Thomas, of Marshfield, Mass.: died 1737.

5. **Judith Ray,** married ———— Hubbard.

6. **Ann Ray,** married Samuel Ward.

7. **Catherine Ray,** married William Greene.

8. **Phœbe Ray,** married John Littlefield.

Account of Simon III Ray.

Removed to New London, Conn., after his father's second marriage; remained a widower 21 years; the last male of his race.

————————

He was a sincere Believer in our Saviour
And by faithful obedience to his Precepts
Duly advanced the Christian Profession.
He died on the 9th of March 1753
In the 85th Year of his age."

SIMON I RAY.

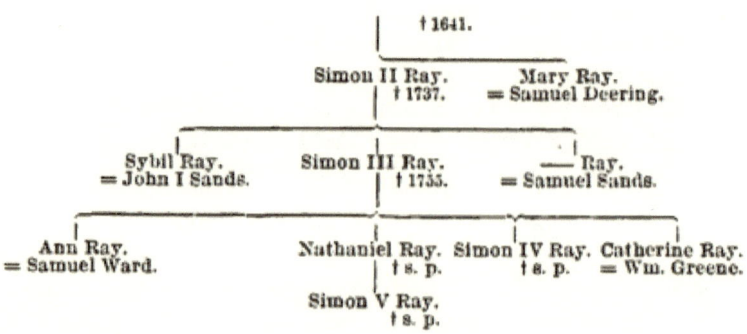

† 1641.

Simon II Ray.   Mary Ray.
        † 1737.   = Samuel Deering.

Sybil Ray.   Simon III Ray.   —— Ray.
= John I Sands.   † 1755.   = Samuel Sands.

Ann Ray.   Nathaniel Ray.   Simon IV Ray.   Catherine Ray.
= Samuel Ward.   † s. p.   † s. p.   = Wm. Greene.

                    Simon V Ray.
                        † s. p.

Appendix.

Copy of a Letter to Henry Ward, then a Boy at School, aged Nine Years, from his Grandmother Catherine, Mrs. William Greene, daughter of Simon III Ray. (PUBLISHED IN THE "MEMORIALS OF MARSHFIELD.")

WARWICK,* March 5th, 1793.

MY father, grandfather, and great grandfather were all named Simon Ray. I shall distinguish them by first, second, and third: Simon Ray 2d came from England with his father, a lad of about sixteen† years, to Plymouth, a very respectable family. Whether his mother came or not, I do not know. But about the time Simon Ray 2d grew up, his father married a widow George, with ten children, which offended him, and he with seven others went to Block Island, and purchased it; and they had but one cow to three families, and they used to catch fish called horse mackerel, and make hasty pudding, and put the milk in as we do molasses; that was their breakfast. They went four mile into the neck to clear the land. At night, when they came home that was their supper, and they all lived in love and harmony like so many good brothers. After a while, a son of the George family, having heard of the purchase of S. Ray 2d had made, came to Block Island to see him. It was rare to see visitors, and being a connection of his father, and he of a benevolent make, and land plenty, told him he would give him half of his purchase if he would clear it, which he readily accepted; and that is the land owned by the Mitchells and Paines at this time.

S. Ray 3d always kept them in fear of dispossessing them; but I believe he gave them a quit claim before he

---

* Warwick, R. I.   † For "sixteen," read "six."

died; I don't know at what age. But when Simon Ray 2d married a Thomas at Marshfield, of a very good family, and brought her to Block Island and had three daughters. Mary, the eldest,* married an Englishman, who carried her to England, and she was the first American lady introduced to the King, and kissed his hand; the second was Saba,† she married a Sands on Long Island, and that family were her offspring, Comfort,‡ and those at Block Island. The 3d was Dorothy, she married a Clapp at Rye, some of them are living, very clever people. Simon Ray 3d was their only son; I don't know his age when his mother died; but although he, S. Ray 2d, was offended, and left his father because he m. a widow with ten children, he married a widow with eleven; and then Simon Ray the 3d left his father and went to New London, and married a Mainwaring; by whom he had a Simon, Gideon, Nathaniel, and Mary. Simon and Gideon were sea-faring men of excellent character; Nathaniel was a tiller of the ground; he had one son, Simon Ray, and died. The son, Simon Ray the 3d, educated at New Haven College. His three sons and grandson all died, I think, between the age of twenty-one and twenty-three years. Their sister Mary went to Marshfield to visit her relations, and there she married into her own family a Thomas; she died young, leaving an only child, Nathaniel Ray. He was left rich; a farm that would cut 100 loads of salt hay, well-stocked house, well furnished with everything. He was educated at Cambridge, and when he was of age it was all wasted but the land. He married Sally Deering of Boston, a charming girl, and your grandma was at the wedding; had sack posset, and a beautiful dressed plumb cake for supper. They had a large family of children; and when the war came he was chosen

---

* Mary was the 2d daughter of Simon II Ray.

† Sybil was the eldest daughter of Simon II Ray, she married John I Sands of Block Island and of Cowneck, L. I.

‡ Comfort Sands of New York, who died in 1834; he was the great grandson of John I Sands and of Sybil Ray.

a mandamus councillor, and being badly advised, accepted it, and went off with the regulars and died at Halifax. His widow lives genteely in that country on a farm. Simon Ray 3d lived a widower twenty-one years; had buried all his sons, and his daughter lived so far from him, that he came to Warwick and married my mother, a maiden lady of thirty-seven years, Deborah Greene, sister to Daniel and Philip Greene, and daughter of Job and Phebe Greene. He was a councillor, had a large landed estate. They went to Block Island, and we had four lovely sisters, Judith, who married a Hubbard; Ann, who married your grandaddy, Samuel Ward; Catherine, your grandma Greene; and Phebe, who married a Littlefield.

Now I must return to Simon Ray 2d. He lived to be 101 years, 1 month and 1 day old. He was blind and lame many years. In the French war a privateer landed and used the inhabitants very ill. He had a chest moved, and they supposed it was money. They tied him to a tree, and whipped him to make him tell, and I think they left him for dead. After he was lame he learned a great deal of the bible by heart; he could say all the Psalms, the New Testament, and a great deal of the Old. My father went in one day and asked him how he did; he said very poorly; for he made it a constant rule to repeat, I've forgot how many Psalms and chapters in a day, and to-day I've only repeated fifty. He asked my father one day how the season was. Oh! said my father, a severe drought, and seemed to repine. He said, my son, let God alone to govern the earth. I just remember him, sitting in an arm chair, with white hair, and being pleasant; and the night he died he called us all to him, and told us to remember our Creator in the days of our youth, and the advantage of living virtuous lives, and making God our friend, and the peace and happiness we should enjoy in the other world. I remember my mother cutting up plain cake and cheese at his funeral, and she cut it in a cheese tub, and it was served in pewter platters; he desired her to do it. You are descended of reputable ancestors on all sides. You had

four grandaddy governors, and that you may be as worthy
man as they all were, is the sincere wish of

Your affectionate grandma,

CATY GREENE.

Extracts from Niles's Narrative. (PUBLISHED MASS. HIST.
SOC., 3d SER., VI.)

"Some time in July, 1689, the French privateer vessels
came to Block Island. . . . In this time they offered great
abuses to Simon Ray,* Esq., an aged gentleman, who lived
somewhat remote in the island, and had not removed his
money nor choicest part of his goods out of his house until
they saw a company of the enemy at a distance coming
thither. He and his son † (who was of the same name, and
after bore the like distinguishing characters of honor and
usefulness that his father had done before, who is now lately
deceased also), as there was no minister in the place, were
wont, in succession, in a truly Christian, laudable manner,
to keep a meeting in their own house on Lord's days, to
pray, sing a suitable portion of the Psalms, and read in
good sermon books, and as they found occasion, to let drop
some words of exhortation in a religious manner on such
as attended their meeting. Upon the sight of the French
coming, the son (then a young man) with the servants carried out some chests, and what they could most readily
convey out of the house and hid them, and themselves also.
When the Frenchmen came into the house, they found only
the old gentleman and his wife; all the rest of the family
were fled. The French demanded his money. He told them
he had none at his command. They observing, by the
signs on the floor, that chests and other things were lately
removed, and the money, which they principally aimed at,

---

* Simon II Ray.   † Simon III Ray.

asked him where they were. He told them he did not know, for his people had carried them out, and he could not tell where they put them. They bid him call his folks, that they might bring them again; which he did, but had no answer, for they were all fled out of hearing.

They being thus disappointed, one of them, in a violent rage, got a piece of rail, and struck him on his head therewith, and in such fury that the blood instantly gushed out and ran on the floor. Upon which his wife took courage, and sharply reprehended them for killing her husband, which she then supposed they had done. Upon this they went off, without the game they expected. After the flow of blood was over, he recovered his health, and lived many years in his former religious usefulness, as before is noted."

THOMAS.

WILLIAM I THOMAS.

Born: in Wales (?) circa 1573.
Died: at Marshfield, Mass., August, 1651; buried there.*
Will:† July 9th, 1651.

Issue.

1. **Nathaniel I Thomas,** of whom later.
2. **Other children.**

---

* In the Marshfield or Winslow burial-ground, his monument, now in fragments, has on it —

> "Here Lyes What Remains
> Of William Thomas Esq
> One of The Founders of
> New Plymouth Colony
> Who Dee^d In ye Month
> Of August 1651 About
> ye 78th Year of
> His Age."

† See N. E. G. & H. Register, IV., 319.

Account of William I Thomas.

Came into the Colony 1640, probably with Rev. Richard Blinman and Hugh Caulkins and others, from Wales or the West of England.

1642 March 17th, freeman.

1642 assistant (with the exception of 1645 and 1646) to the time of his death. *

NATHANIEL I THOMAS.

Born: in Wales (?) circa 1606.

Died: at Marshfield, Mass., February 13th 1674; buried there † on the 16th of the same month.

Married: ———. ‡

Issue.

1. **William II Thomas,** of Marshfield, born in England 1638; died unmarried March, 1718.

---

* Secretary Morton says of him: "1651, This year Mr. William Thomas expired his natural life in much comfort. He served in the place of magistracy divers years; he was a well approved and well grounded Christian; well read in the Holy Scriptures and other approved authors; a good lover and approver of godly ministers and good Christians, and one that had a sincere desire to promote the common good, both of church and state. He died of consumption, and was honorably buried at Marshfield."

† In the Marshfield or Winslow burial-ground, his monument bears the following inscription:

"Here Lyes The
Remains of
Nathaniel Thomas
Gent Who Dec^d
ye 13th Day of February
1674 about ye 68th Year
Of His Age."

‡ Mentioned in the Will of William I Thomas.

2. **Nathaniel II Thomas**, born in this country 1643; died October 1718; left issue male.

3. **Mary Thomas**, married 1661, Simon II Ray.

4. **Elizabeth Thomas**, born 1646.

5. **Dorothy Thomas**.

Account of Nathaniel I Thomas.

Came over with his father in 1640, bringing wife and son William II; on his father's death he succeeded to the homestead.

1643 Lieutenant of a troop.

1644 Freeman.

WILLIAM I THOMAS.
† 1651.

Nathaniel Thomas.
† 1674.

| William II Thomas. † 1718. s. p. | Nathaniel II Thomas. † 1718. left issue male. | Mary Thomas. = Simon II Ray. | Elizabeth Thomas. | Dorothy Thomas. |

GUTHRIE.

ROBERT GUTHRIE.

Died: on Block Island, December 3d 1692; buried in the graveyard on Block Island.*

Married: 1st Margaret———; born 1633; died on Block Island April 5th 1687; buried there.†

——— 2dly. June 5th 1689, Anna, daughter of Dr. John Alcock,‡ and of Sarah Palgrave his wife; baptized Boston, Mass., May 26th 1650; married§ 1st 1670 John Williams, of Boston; left a widow at Newport, R. I. 1688.

---

* fide S. R. Sands (1878): he was buried alongside of his 1st wife; his gravestone has sunk into the ground.

† Her tombstone bears the following epitaph:

> "Here lieth
> The body of M
> Margret Gvtry
> Aged 54 years who
> Departed this
> Life April 5 1687."

‡ For account of the Alcock family see page 50.

§ For marriage contract with John Williams, see Records of Boston, Liber. VI, 241; see page 62.

Issue.

1. **Catherine Guthrie,** born on Block Island June 24th 1690; married at Newport, R. I., September 9th 1706 John II Sands; died at Cowneck, L. I., February 10th 1769; buried there in the Sands graveyard.

Account of Robert Guthrie.

Robert Guthrie, Gutterege, Guttarage, Gutry, of Edinborough, Scotland, was one of the early settlers on Block Island.

1670–1671 Tax-rater on Block Island.

1687 Overseer of the Poor on Block Island.

ALCOCK.

GEORGE ALCOCK.

Born: in England.
Died: at Roxbury, Mass., December 30th 1640.
Will: * December 22d 1640.
Married: 1st in England, ——Hooker (sister to Rev. Thomas Hooker, who was born at Marfield, co. Leicester, England, circa 1586); died at Roxbury, Mass., 1630.

—— 2dly. In England, Elizabeth ——; she married again, April 1641, Henry Dingham, of Watertown, Mass., a surgeon.

Issue.

1. **John Alcock,** of whom later.
2. **Samuel Alcock,** born April 16th 1637; graduated at Harvard 1659; a physician; died 1677; left a widow, but no children.

---

* N. E. G. Register, II. 104; see page 61.

Account of George Alcock.

He was a physician at Roxbury, who came over in the fleet with Governor Winthrop in 1630, bringing with him his first wife, who died not long afterwards; applied for admission as freeman October 19th 1630, admitted as such May 18th 1631; deacon at Dorchester; representative at the first court held May 14th 1634, as well as on other occasions, deacon at Roxbury. He went back to England to bring his son John to America, and during this visit, or the next, he married his second wife. The church record on the occasion of his death, says: "He left a good name behind him, the poor of the church much bewailing his loss."

His homestead in Roxbury, consisting of 5 acres, was situated on the south side of Bartlett street, near Lambert, having Thomas Dudley on the north, John Dane on the south, a highway on the east and the meeting-house common on the west; it passed to the heirs of Joshua Lamb, who married May Alcock, his granddaughter.

He also owned 20 acres of upland and marsh on the east side of the Neck, extending from the line near the "Bull pasture" to the burying-ground; this also passed to the representatives of his granddaughter, Mrs. Lamb.

The colonists who settled at Roxbury came mostly from London and its vicinity and from Nazing, a village in Essex; a few came from the West of England; they were people of substance, many of them farmers, none being of the poorer sort.

JOHN ALCOCK.

Born: in England, 1627.

Died: Boston, March 27th 1667; buried at Roxbury March 29th.

Will: May 10th 1666.

Married: Sarah, daughter of Dr. Richard Palgrave *
of Charlestown; born in England in 1621; died in Roxbury November 27th 1665.

Issue.

1. **Joanna Alcock,** born 1649; died young.
2. **Anna Alcock,** baptized May 26th 1650; married †
1st 1670, John Williams of Boston, left a widow at Newport, R. I., 1688; married again June 5th 1689 to Robert
Guthrie of Block Island.
3. **Sarah Alcock,** twin sister of Anna, baptized at the
same time; married 1670 Rev. Zachariah Whitman.
4. **Mary Alcock,** born August 15th 1652; married
Joshua Lamb of Roxbury.
5. **George Alcock,** born March 25th 1655; graduated
at Harvard 1673; died in London; will of February 27th
1677, proved March 9th 1677 at Doctor's Commons.
6. **John Alcock,** born 5th, baptized 15th of March
1657; died unmarried May 5 1690; buried at Roxbury in
the old burying-ground, corner of Washington and Eustis
streets. ‡
7. **Elizabeth Alcock,** baptized March 27th 1659.
8. **Joanna Alcock,** born May 6th 1660.
9. **Palgrave Alcock,** born July 20th 1662; of Roxbury;
died November 24th 1710; will proved December 14th
1710; left widow, but no issue.

Account of John Alcock.

Born in England; remained there when his father first
came to this country in 1630; he accompanied his father to

---

* For account of Palgrave family see page 66.

† For marriage contract with John Williams, see Records of Boston,
Liber VI. 241; see page 62.

‡ His tombstone has on it the following epitaph: "John Alcocke,
May 5, 1690, in ye 35th year of his age."

Massachusetts on a subsequent voyage: graduated at Harvard 1646; taught school at Hartford 1647–1648; this probably under the influence of his mother's brother, the Rev. Thomas Hooker, who was settled there: freeman November 12th 1652; established himself as a physician at Roxbury, but subsequently removed to Boston, probably prior to 1657; several of his children were born in Boston, but they were all carried to Roxbury for baptism; was employed on public service to locate grants of land; as a retribution, he received a grant of land of one thousand acres, now included in the town of Marlborough and known as "The Farm"; he had also other grants of land; he owned land on Boston Neck, at Dorchester, on the Assabet River, in Stow, and the estate known as the "Williams Place," in Scituate, near the harbor; he was identified with the settlement of Block Island.

GEORGE ALCOCK.
†1640.

John Alcock.
†1667.

Samuel Alcock.
†1677. s. p.

Joanna Alcock.
†young.

Anna Alcock.
=J. Williams.
=R. Guthrie.

Sarah Alcock.
=Z. Whitman.

Mary Alcock.
=J. Lamb.

George Alcock.
†in London.

Elizabeth Alcock.

Joanna Alcock.

Falgrave Alcock.
†1710. s. p.

Appendix.

Abstract of Will of George Alcock. (GEN. REG. II. 104.)

22 day 11th, called December, Anno Domini 1640.

The last Will & Testament wch I George Alcock of Roxbury in N: E: doe make, havinge yet my perfect vnderstandinge and memory according to the measure thereof.

Debts to be paid both in owld England & in new. My debt of 40£. to my sonne John, wch I have of his in my hands.— Wife to have £100, to be paid her in whatsoever she shall chuse.— Brother Thomas Alcocke of Dedham all that he oweth me, & my Heifer wch is wth calfe, wh came of the great Cow, if my goodes will howld out, else he shall have only hir Calfe, & I give his 2 children each of them 2.^{lb.} To our brother Edward Porter, 20 bushles of Indian Corne, & to our brother Chandler, the monye he oweth me.— To Elizabeth Blandfeild 2¹, she shall (be) put forth where she may be well educated.— To my servant Joseph Wise, my young heifer, & the rest of his time, from after mid-somer next.— To my servant, John Plimton, his time from after midsomer, for 5¹ — My youngest sone shall have the silver bowles, & my wife the silver spoons.— My house and lands to be improved for the best, for the education of my children, and the halfe of ye revenue of the farme shall be to educate my sone John in learninge, together wth the wisest improvement of his 40¹ — The other half to educate sone Samuell, for 7 yeares, beginning from ye 1st daye of ye 11 month, called January, about wch time expired, my sone John will be 21 yeares of age.— Part of the debts to my brother Carwithy be layde out on the 2 Cowes I had of Mr Perkins.— My lovinge brethren, Phillip

Eliot & William Park be my executors.   My brother Mr
Hooker, Mr Welde, Mr Eliot, Isaac Heath to overseers.

                                GEORGE ALCOCKE.

Witnesses
    Tho Welde
    Thom Alcocke
    (28) 11 : 1640.

Articles of Agreement on a Contract of Marriage between Anna Alcock, Daughter of Dr. John Alcock, and John Williams, Jan. 25, 1669, 70.   (RECORD OFFICE OF DEEDS, SUFFOLK CO., MASS., LIBER VI., FOL. 241.)

Articles of agreement on a contract of marriage, by God's
permission, to bee solemnized, in convenient time, by &
betweene John Williams, the sonn of the late Nathaniell
Williams, of Boston, in the Countie of Suffolke of the Massachusetts Colony in New England, glower & Anna Alcock,
eldest daughter of the late John Alcock of Roxbury in the
same Countie and Colony in New England, phissision had
made drawne & concluded upon this 25th of January, 1669,
by & betweene the sajd John Williams on the one part, &
the sajd Anna of Boston aforesajd, and Samuell Alcock,
unckle to the sajd Anna of Boston aforesajd, phisisian,
ffeoffes in trust for the sajd Anna Alcock, on the other part
in manner & forme as followeth, vizt : imprimis the sajd
John Williams for himselfe, his heirs, executoʳ, administratoʳ, & assigns, doth hereby firmly couenant, promise,
& grant, and hereby doth freely, fully & absolutely bind &
engage himselfe, & his heires, executoʳ, administratoʳ, &
assigns, to the above mentioned Anna Alcock, Edward Rawson & Samuell Alcock ffeoffes aforesajd to & on the behalfe
of the said Anna Alcock, her heires, executoʳ, administratoʳ
& assignes, that hee the sajd John Williams, his heires,
executoʳ, administratoʳ, & assigns, shall & will from time
to time & at all times saue & defend & forever secure Edward
Rawson above mentioned, & John Hull of Boston, & their

heires executo' administrato' & assignes, & all & euery of them
respectively of & from all & all manner of suites, debts,
claymes & demands, from all persons & and euery person
whatsoeuer, clayming or that shall clayme any due, debt,
right, title, or interest, to or from the estate of the late Anna
Palfgrave, or any part thereof, to whose last will & testament bearing date the eleaneth of March, 1668–9, they the
said Edward Rawson & John Hull are executo', and haue
delivered up the same & euery part thereof to the sajd
Annah Alcock, & that they the said Edward Rawson &
John Hull & their respective heires, executo' administrato' & assignes shall bee the better secured from all dam-
mages or any dammage, that shall or may accrue vnto them,
or any of them by virtue of the sajd executorship, they the
sajd John Williams & Anna Alcock his intended wife, doe
hereby either of themselves firmly bind & make over, the
dwelling house in Boston, now in the possession of Thomas
Bingly given unto the sajd Anna Alcock, as by the tearmes
in the sajd last of the sajd late Anna Palsgrave, is ex-
pressed to him the said Edward Rawson & John Hull, their
& every of their respective heires, executo', administrato'
& assignes, that soe her just debts & legacies due to one to
another, to all persons whatsoever, may bee fully pajd &
truly made good to all intents & purposes whatsoeuer. It
is further agreed & concluded vpon by & betweene the
parties first above mentioned, & the sajd John Williams
doth couenant, promise & grant to & with the sajd Edward
Rawson & Samuell Alcock ffeoffees aforesajd that hee the
sajd John Williams shall not during the life of the sajd
Anna his intended wife or the life of any of the heires of
her body, sell or convey away the above mentioned dwelling
house of the late Anna Palsgrave in Boston or the land
about it, or any part thereof belonging thereunto, but that
the same shall come & decend & foreuer bee unto the sajd
Anna & to the heire or heires of the said Anna, by him the
sajd John Williams in case shee the said Anna shall dye
before the sajd John, for them to enjoy next & immediately
after his & her decease forever. It is further agreed & concluded by & betweene the parties above mentioned, and the

sajd John Williams for himself his heires, executo', administrato', & assignes doth hereby couenant, promise, & grant to & with the said Edward Rawson & Samuell Alcock ffeoffees aforesajd their & euery of their respective heires, executo', administrato', & assignes that the third part of the farme of vpland & meadow of the late John Alcock situate, lying & being at a place called Assibath about & on both sides of the riuer, part whereof being still in the occupation of Thomas Hedge, when divided & parted according to the last will of the late John Alcock, bearing date the 10th of May 1666, betweene the sajd Anna, & Sarah, & Mary, daughters of the sajd late John Alcock, to whome he gaue the same by equall shares, shall be improued by him the sajd John Williams, to & for his & her the sajd Anna' best advantage, during their naturall liues, but after his the sajd John Williams death, in case hee out liue the sajd Anna his intended wife, the sajd third part of that farme shall also after the death of the sajd John immediatly bee & goe vnto the heire & heires of the sajd John, borne of the sajd Annah, & for want of such heire or heires, then to the heires of John Alcock aforenamed, vizt: Sarah & Mary, sisters of the sajd Anna, for that the will of the sajd John Alcock seemes to giue the same as the heires of the sajd Anna should also in case of want of naturall heires from the said Sarah & Mary Alcock alike, bee heires to them as by virtue of their said ffathers will is or was intended, & before the division of the sajd ffarme the sajd John shall enjoy his intended wiues third part of the profits or bennifits that shall or may arise from the improvement of the sd farme, & the stock thereupon & vnto them belonging in common, together with such surplusage as shall bee & grow due, to him in right of the sajd Anna his intended wife from the estate of the sajd late John Alcock her sajd late ffather, forasmuch as this farme at Assibath is but part of the estate of the sajd late John Alcock, & his whole estate is to be divided amongst all his children, proportions excepting a dubble portion thereof which at right belongeth vnto the eldest soun of the sajd late John Alcock that shall liue &

come to the full age of one & twenty yeares, which hee then must haue, enjoy, & fully dispose of foreuer. The sajd John Williams for the true & lawfull of all & euery the above written articles, declarations, grants, couenants & agreements, doth hereby absolutely & firmly engage & bind himselfe & his heirs, executo', administrato', & assignes, & euevery of them in the penall sume of ffive hundred pounds of starling money of New England, to bee forfeited & pajd vnto the aforenamed Edward Rawson & Samuell Alcock ffeoffees & trustees aforesajd, their heires, executo', administrato', & assignes for the proper & only vse & behoofe of the sajd Anna his intended wife & her heires, executo', administrato', & assignes, foreuer. In witness whereof the sajd parties, vizt: John Williams & the sajd Anna Alcock his intended wife, with Edward Rawson & Samuell Alcock ffeoffees & trustees aforesajd, haue hereunto interchangably set their hands & seales this sajd twenty ffifth day of January, in the twenty & first yeare of the Reigne of our Soueraigne Lord Charles the Second by the Grace of God, King of England, Scotland, ffrance & Ireland & yeare of our Lord one thousand six hundred sixty & nine 1669

———
70

JOHN WILLIAMS L s

Signed sealed & delivered
  in the presents of vs:

    JOHN GREENE
    WILLIAM RAWSON
    MARY TORY

The name John at the beginning of the third line & sajd interlined in the fourth line — aboue written were there soe placed before the signing, sealing and deliuery hereof. JOHN GREENE, WILLIAM RAWSON, MARY TORREY. —— This instrument was acknowledged by John Williams to bee his act & deed, 15th of ffeb. 1669. before me.
    JOHN LENCRET, Assist. ———

5

PALGRAVE.

RICHARD PALGRAVE.

Died: Charlestown, Mass., 1656.

Married: in England, Anne ——; after her husband's death removed to Roxbury, and resided with her son-in-law, Dr. John Alcock; died in Roxbury, and buried there March 17th 1668–69, aged 75 years; will of March 11th 1668–69, mentions among others the children of her deceased daughter, Mrs. Alcock.

Issue.

1. **Mary Palgrave,** born in England; married Roger Wellington.

2. **Sarah Palgrave,** born in England 1621; married Dr. John Alcock; died November 27th 1665.

3. **Rebecca Palgrave,** born in Boston July 25th 1631.

4. **John Palgrave,** born March 6th 1634; baptized in Boston on the 9th of the same month.

5. **Lydia Palgrave,** born January 15th 1635; baptized in Boston on the 17th of the same month; married Edmund Heylett of Stepney, near London.

6. **Bethia Palgrave,** baptized in Boston July 8th 1638; died August 21st 1638.

Account of Richard Palgrave.

Richard Palgrave or Palsgrave came over in the fleet with Winthrop in 1630; came from Stepney, co. Middlesex, bringing with him his wife and his daughters, Mary and Sarah; the first medical man established in Charlestown; member of the Boston church with his wife, Nos. 105 and 106; they did not transfer their relation to Charlestown; requested admission as freeman October 19th 1630, took the oath May 18th 1631.

RICHARD PALGRAVE.
† 1656.

Mary Palgrave.	Sarah Palgrave.	Rebecca Palgrave.	John Palgrave.	Lydia Palgrave.	Bethia Palgrave.
= R. Wellington.	† 1665.			= E. Heylett.	† 1638.
	= John Alcock.				

CORNELL.

JOHN I CORNELL.

Died: —— interred in the Cornell graveyard* on Cow-neck, L. I.

Married: Mary Russel.

Issue.

1. **Richard I Cornell,** born 1675; married Hannah Thorne of Flushing; left issue.

2. **Joshua I Cornell,** born 1677; married Sarah Thorne, the sister of the above; left issue.

3. **John II Cornell,** born 1681; married —— Starr, of Danbury, Conn.; left issue.

4. **Caleb I Cornell,** of whom later.

5. **Mary Cornell,** born 1679; married 1697 James II Sands of Mattinecock, L. I.

---

* The Cornell graveyard is near the Isaac Dodge or Treadwell house, in the outskirts of Port Washington, Cowneck, L. I.

6. **Rebecca Cornell,** born 1685; married Comfort Starr of Danbury, Conn.

Account of John I Cornell.

John I Cornell or Cornwell, came from England circa 1655; about the year 1677 he settled on Cowneck, L. I., with his wife and sons Richard I and Joshua I, and purchased or patented land, which included the farm occupied later by Henry Sands, and he gave half an acre for a burial place for the family; 1702 he and his sons purchased of Thomas Willet, for £600, the farm on which John Williams and Caleb Cornell lived, adjoining the land of Thomas Barker.

CALEB I CORNELL.

Born: on Cowneck, 1683.
Died: on Cowneck, ——
Married: October 10th 1705, Elizabeth Hagner of Flushing, L. I., died 1734.

Issue.

1. **Richardson Cornell,** born July 16th 1706; died unmarried.

2. **Caleb II Cornell,** born March 28th 1709; died December 16th 1784; left a son who died unmarried.

3. **Elizabeth Cornell,** born September 27th 1711; married John III Sands.

4. **Mary Cornell,** born June 19th 1714; married Thomas Appleby; died December 23d 1780.

5. **John III Cornell,** born October 26th 1716; died January 8th 1790.

6. **Susanna Cornell,** died young.

7. **Richard II Cornell,** born May 10th 1720; died circa 1772.

8. **William Cornell**, born September 15th 1721; died November 5th 1797.

9. **Joshua II Cornell**, born May 10th 1726; died June 20th 1800.

10. **Margaret Cornell**, born February 28th 1728; married John Willis; died December 16th 1808.

———

JOHN I CORNELL.
= Mary Russell.

- Richard I Cornell. left issue.
  - Richardson Cornell. † s. p.
  - Caleb II Cornell. † s. p.
  - Elizabeth Cornell. = John III Sands.
  - Mary Cornell. = Thos. Appleby.
- Joshua I Cornell. left issue.
- John II Cornell. left issue.
  - John III Cornell. † 1790.
  - Susan Cornell. † young.
- Caleb I Cornell. = Elizabeth Hagner.
  - Richard II Cornell.
- Mary Cornell. = James II Sands.
  - William Cornell. † 1797.
  - Joshua II Cornell. † 1800.
- Rebecca Cornell. = Comfort Starr.
  - Margaret Cornell. = John Willis.

DODGE.

TRISTRAM I DODGE.

Died: on Block Island 1700—1710.
Will: intestate.

Issue.

1. Israel Dodge.
2. John Dodge.
3. **William I Dodge,** of whom later.
4. Tristram II Dodge.

Account of Tristram I Dodge.

Sailed from Taunton, Mass., 1661, and settled on Block Island.

WILLIAM I DODGE.

Died: on Block Island.
Will: intestate.

Issue.

1. **William II Dodge,** born on Block Island, March 8th 1680.
2. **Elizabeth Dodge,** born on Block Island, May 1683.
3. **Samuel I Dodge,** of whom later.

SAMUEL I DODGE.

Born: on Block Island, September 19th 1691.
Died: during or before 1766; buried on Cowneck, L. I., probably on or near Richard Mott's place.
Married: Elizabeth ——
Will: May 23d 1761;* proved New York, 1766; recorded Surrogate's Office, N. Y. Co., Liber 23, fol. 28.

Issue.

1. **Jeremiah Dodge.**
2. **Samuel II Dodge.**
3. **Wilkie I Dodge,** of whom later.

WILKIE I DODGE.

Born: on Cowneck, L. I.
Died: on Cowneck, 1752; interred there in the graveyard of the Quaker Meeting House.
Married: Mary, daughter of Thomas III Hunt,† of Hunt's Point, Westchester Co., N. Y., by Sarah Ward his

---

* See page 77.
† For account of Hunt family see page 78.

wife; born at Hunt's Point, 1725; died in New York, July 22d 1796; interred in the vault of Comfort Sands, Nassau Street, N. Y., in the Middle Dutch Church; remains removed 1845, to St. Paul's Church, Eastchester, Westchester Co., N. Y.

Will: February 13th 1752;* recorded Surrogate's Office, N. Y. Co., Liber 18, fol. 148.

Issue.

1. **Samuel III Dodge**, died in New Jersey; married Deborah, daughter of Robert North; she died in New York.

2. **Sarah Dodge**, born at Hunt's Point, 1749; married June 3d, 1769, Comfort Sands.

3. **Jesse Dodge**, alive in 1752.

4. **Wilkie II Dodge**, posthumous; master of a vessel during the Revolution, taken prisoner and died in N. Y. about 1778.

Account of Wilkie I Dodge.

A ship carpenter by trade; lived at Whitestone until a little before his death, when he moved to Cowneck; his widow and children remained at Cowneck for a while after his death; his widow then went to her mother's at Hunt's Point, and remained there till 1760 or 1762; she then moved to New York with her family, and kept for three or four years a small retail shop opposite Walton's in Queen (now Pearl) Street; her sons went out to trades, Samuel III Dodge with Ward Hunt a joiner, and Wilkie II with Joseph Gregg a brassfounder; she then broke up her shop and she and her daughter lived with Joseph Drake in Peck Slip, until her daughter's marriage with Comfort Sands; she then lived with them until her death.

---

* See page 77.

TRISTRAM I DODGE.

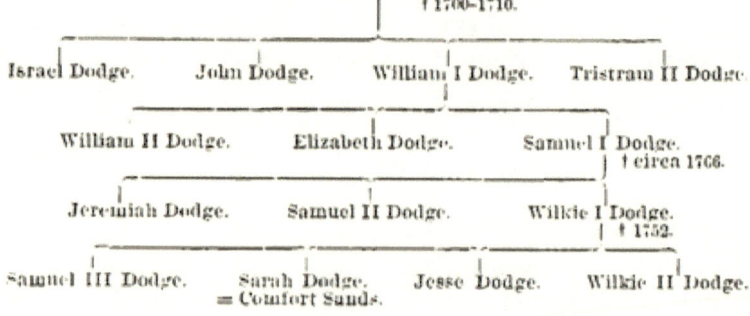

† 1700–1710.

Israel Dodge.   John Dodge.   William I Dodge.   Tristram II Dodge.

William II Dodge.   Elizabeth Dodge.   Samuel I Dodge.
                                                         † circa 1766.

Jeremiah Dodge.   Samuel II Dodge.   Wilkie I Dodge.
                                                         † 1752.

Samuel III Dodge.   Sarah Dodge.   Jesse Dodge.   Wilkie II Dodge.
                         = Comfort Sands.

Appendix.

Abstract of Will of Samuel I Dodge.— RECORDED OFF. OF SUR-
ROGATE OF THE COUNTY OF N. Y., LIBER 23, FOL. 28.

Proved, N. Y., 1766. Dated May 23, 1761.

1. Bequests for her life to his wife Elizabeth.

2. Lot of land in Queen Street, N. Y., to his son Jeremiah,
the next lot of land to his son Samuel.

3. His whole estate (except as above and as follows) to
his said two sons and daughter Deborah.

4. To his grandson, Samuel son of Wilkie, deceased, all
the ground in Cowneck, L. I., near the house of Joseph
Dodge, lying on the south side of the road that leads from
said house up the Neck between said road and the farm of
Oliver Baxter, be it more or less.

Abstract of Will of Wilkie I Dodge.— RECORDED OFF. OF SUR-
ROGATE OF THE COUNTY OF N. Y., LIBER 18, FOL. 148.

Dated feb. 13 1752.

Wilkie Dodge of Flushing, Queens co. Nassau Isl⁴, Province of N. Y.

1ˢᵗ "to my son Samuel, lot of land on Cow neck, Nassau
Isl⁴, near the land of my father joining to the Creek." Be-
queathes " to his daughter Sarah and to his youngest son
Jesse, each certain silver plate : appoints as executors his
father, Samuel Dodge, and his brother, Samuel Dodge, and
Mary Dodge his wife."

HUNT.

THOMAS I HUNT.

(OF THE GROVE FARM, WESTCHESTER CO., N. Y.)

Died: October 6th 1694.

Will: October 6th 1694; proved February 27th 1695; recorded in the Surrogate's Office, N. Y., Liber 5, fol. 73.*

Married: prior to August 6th 1666, Elizabeth,† daughter of Edward I Jessop, of Westchester Co., N. Y.

Issue.

1. **Thomas II Hunt,** of whom later.
2. **Josiah Hunt,** married Berthia Horguson; left son Josiah, upon whom his grandfather, Thomas I Hunt, by will, entailed the Grove Farm.

---

* See page 84.

† The landed wealth of this family dates from this marriage; for account of Jessop family, see p. 87.

3. **Joseph Hunt**, alive 1729; left issue male.
4. **John Hunt**, alive 1709; left issue male.
5. **Abigail Hunt**.
6. **Mary Hunt**, born prior to 1666.

Account of Thomas I Hunt.

1652 Shortly after this time bought land of Augustine Hemans, on Throckmorton's Neck, Westchester Co., N. Y.

1663 Freeman at the General Court of Connecticut.

1664 October, representative in Connecticut.

1665 September 3d, complaint lodged by him at the Westchester Town Court against an Indian.

1670 Accusation by him and another man against Katherine Harryson for witchcraft.

1683 Representative from Westchester at the Assembly at Jamaica, L. I.

THOMAS II HUNT.

(OF HUNT'S POINT, WESTCHESTER CO., N. Y.)

Died: October 25th 1739.
Will: January 7th 1711.
Married: Elizabeth, daughter of —— Gardiner; born 1667; died 1724.

Issue.

1. **Thomas III Hunt**, of whom later.
2. **Lewis Hunt.**
3. **Robert Hunt**, died 1749.

4. **Abigail Hunt.**

5. **Augustine Hunt,** born September 15th 1716; died March 24th 1809.

Account of Thomas II Hunt.

1692 Trustee of Westchester town.

1702, 1709 Vestryman of St. Peter's Church, Westchester, N. Y.

THOMAS III HUNT.

(OF HUNT'S POINT.)

Born : circa 1700.

Died : 1749.

Will : intestate; his real estate went by descent to his eldest son, Thomas IV Hunt.

Married : Sarah, daughter of —— Ward; died circa 1765.

Issue.

1. **Thomas IV Hunt,** born 1723; married a daughter of Joseph Wright, of Flushing; died July 4th 1808; inherited Hunt's Point.

2. **Mary Hunt,** born 1725; married Wilkie I Dodge, of Cowneck, L. I.; died July 22d 1796.

3. **Jesse Hunt,** born 1727; married Sarah Staples, of Fairfield, Conn.

4. **Meriam Hunt,** born 1730; married John Field, of Dutchess Co., N. Y.

5. **Phebe Hunt,** born 1733; married Joseph Drake, of Eastchester, Westchester Co., N. Y.

6. **Sarah Hunt,** born 1736; married Solomon Fowler, of Eastchester, Westchester Co., N. Y.

7. **Ward Hunt,** born 1739; married —— Briggs, of Eastchester, Westchester Co., N. Y.

Account of Thomas III Hunt.

1729 Trustee of St. Peter's Church, Westchester, N. Y.
1729, 1730 Alderman of Westchester, N. Y.

THOMAS I HUNT.
† 1694.

| Joseph Hunt. left issue male. | John Hunt. left issue male. | Abigail Hunt. | Mary Hunt. |

Thomas II Hunt. † 1739.
Josiah Hunt. line extinct in the males.

Augustine Hunt. † 1800.

Thomas III Hunt. † 1749.
Lewis Hunt.
Robert Hunt. † 1749.
Abigail Hunt.

Thomas IV Hunt. † 1808.
Mary Hunt. = Willie I Dodge.
Jesse Hunt. = Sarah Staples.
Meriam Hunt. = John Field.
Phebe Hunt. = Joseph Drake.
Sarah Hunt. = Solomon Fowler.
Ward Hunt. = —— Briggs.

Appendix.

The Grove Farm, Westchester Co., N. Y.

The "Grove Farm," patented * originally, December 4th, 1667, and confirmed subsequently by patent of the 12th of January, 1686, in favor of Thomas I Hunt, consisted of Spicer's and Brockett's Necks, which are situated on the south-west extremity of Throckmorton's Neck proper.

Thomas I Hunt, on his death, 1694, left the Grove Farm to his grandson, Josiah Hunt, the son of his 2d son Josiah; on the death of Josiah it passed to his son Thomas; and on his death 1756, it went to his eldest daughter Mianna Hunt, who married Elijah Ferris, and whose sons, John H., William and Charlton Ferris, owned it in 1848.

The mansion, erected in 1697, prettily situated at the entrance of Spicer's Creek, on the border of Westchester Creek, is surrounded by old locusts.

Hunt's Point, Westchester Co., N. Y.

Hunt's Point, situated at the south-east extremity of the Great Planting Rock, called by the Indians Quinnahung, in the village of Westfarms, came into the Hunt family through the Jessop alliance; it was granted to Thomas II Hunt by his father in 1688. It is now the property of Daniel Winship (1842), who married the widow of Richard Hunt. There is a family graveyard on this place.

---

* The original patent, which in 1848 was in the possession of Charlton Ferris, has been published in Bolton II. 149.

Will of Thomas I Hunt. (SURROGATE'S OFFICE, N. Y., LIBER 5, FOL. 73.)

In the name of God, Amen.

I Thomas Hunt Senr. of ye Grove ffarme In Westchester County & Collony of New Yorke being att this time weak of body but of perfect Memory throigh Marcy am Resolved to make this my Last will and Testam't in order to settle and distribute my Estate as hereafter followeth to prevent all Discord and trouble that might otherwise arise amongst my children for want thereof Revoking all former wills and Declaring them to be void and of none Effect and this to remain in full force & virtue.

Imprimis I give my soul to God that gave it me and my boddy to be decently burried. Item I will that all Debts which are Justly due from me to any person or persons whatsoever be first payd out of my out of my Living Stock as Cattle and other Creatures. Item I give and bequeath unto my Grand sonn Josiah Hunt Eldest son of my son Josiah Hunt and unto his heirs male Lawfully begotten all my lands and meadows known by or called by the name of ye Grove ffarme aforesaid as Mentioned in my pattent Granted by Governor Nicolls Dated the fforth day of December one thousand six hundred sixty seven together with all and singular my houses, orchards and other Improvements thereon with all and singular my household stuff and carts plows and all other utensills for Husbandry as Likewise all my Carpenters tools and arms Together with all my Living stock of creatures of what kind soever and also all my corn of what sort soever and ye sider which shall bee found in my seller att my Decease all the before Recited Goods & Chattels I give and bequeath unto my Grandson Josiah Hunt aforesaid his heirs & assigns forever I Doe hereby Entail and Confirme the said Lands Meadows & Improvements unto my said Grandson Josiah Hunt Eldest sonn of my sonn Josiah Hunt and his heirs male Lawfully begotten and to his male heirs from Generation to Generation forever that no part or parcell thereof shall be sould made away or Dispossed off nor the property, altered contrary to this my will. But to continue according to the plaine Intent and true meaning of these Express words without any collution fraud or deceit and the said Lands and premises to continue a firme Entaild Estate to my said Grandson Josiah Hunt Eldest son of my son Josiah Hunt and his issue male Lawfully begotten for Ever Declaring my sonn Josiah Hunt to be sole Executor of this my Last Will and Testament to succeed me in possession & Enjoym't of the Grove ffarm before Expresst for and in the behalf of my Grandson Josiah Hunt aforesaid Provided always that if my Grandson Josiah Hunt aforesaid should dye without any Issue male Lawfully begotten then his next survivant brother shall possess and Enjoy the said Lands & others the premises in manner & form as before Expresst. Item. I give & bequeath unto my four sons Thomas Hunt Joseph Hunt John Hunt & Josiah Hunt the sume of fourty pounds that is to say to my son Thomas Hunt Ten pounds Joseph Hunt Ten pounds John Hunt Ten pounds & Josiah Hunt ten pounds to be paid within one year after my Decease.

Item. I give and bequeath unto my Daughter Abigail Pinkney ten pounds to be payd her within one year after my Decease in Cloath belonging to her mother as they shall be apprized by two Indifferent men.

Item. I give and bequeath unto my Grand daughter Abigail Hunt Daughter of my sonn Thomas Hunt one feather bed & two blankets.

Item. I give and bequeath unto my grant Daughter Abigail Hunt daughter of my son Josiah Hunt one feather bed & two blanketts. Item. I give and bequeath to my Grand Daughter Martha Hunt Daughter of my sonn Joseph Hunt four sheep.

Item. I will also that my negro man named Mingo shall live upon the Grove Ffarm the full term of seven years after my Decease and att ye Expiration of seven years as aforesaid to be sett free from his servitude for Ever and the negro Child named Sarah which is borne in my house I bequeath unto my son Joseph Hunt to Live with him or his heirs until she comes to the age of five and twenty years and then to be free from her servitude for Ever.

Lastly. I Desire authorize and appoint my Ffriends William Lawrence of Flushing and Thomas Stevenson of New Town to be my Overseers and Executors in trust to see this my Last will & Testam-t punctually performed and fullfilled. In Witness whereof I the said Thomas Hunt Senr. have hereunto putt to my hand and seale this sixt day of Octob in the year of our Lord one thousand six hundred ninety ffour the mark of Tho, (mark) Hunt (seale).

David Jamison D. Secry. Signed sealed & perfected in presence of us Robert Hustett, Joseph Havilalent, Edward Collier.

JESSOP.

EDWARD I JESSOP.

Died: Westchester, N. Y., 1666.

Will: August 6th 1666; proved Flushing, November 14th 1666; recorded in the Surrogate's Office, N. Y., Liber I, fol. 14.*

Married: 1st. —— daughter of John I Whitmore,† of Stamford, Conn.

—— 2d. Elizabeth, daughter of —— Bridges; alive,‡ June, 1668.

Issue.

1. **Elizabeth Jessop,** married prior to August 1666, Thomas I Hunt of the Grove, Westchester, N. Y.

2. **Hannah Jessop,** not 18 in 1666.

3. **Edward II Jessop,** a minor in 1666.

---

* See page 89.

† For account of Whitmore see page 90.

‡ In June 20th 1668, her name is attached to a deed of sale to Thomas Hunt, see Bolton II. 262.

Account of Edward I Jessop.

1641–1650 At Stamford, Conn.

1653 Owned lands on Sascoe Creek, Fairfield Co., Conn.

1656 Middleburg, L. I., N. Y.

1662 Newtown, L. I., N. Y.

1664–1666 Westchester, N. Y.

1665 Deputy from Westchester to Hempstead, L. I.

1666 Owned with John Richardson the land now occupied by Westfarms, N. Y.

Appendix.

Will of Edward I Jessop. (SURROGATE'S OFFICE, N. Y., LIBER I, FOL. 14.)

Being sicke and weake in body, yet in perfect memory, I bequeath my soule to ye Almighty God that gave it, and my body after my death to be decently buried, my funeral to be discharged, and my debts to be paid. I will and bequeath to my daughter, Elizabeth Hunt, twenty shillings, besides which I have already given her to be paid in a year and a day after my decease. I will and bequeath unto my daughter, Hannah Jessop, the sum of five and thirty pounds with that she hath already, to be paid unto her at eighteen years of age.

I will and bequeath unto my sonne, Edward Jessup, two mares with two colts by their sides; one is a gray mare, and the other is a mare marked on both ears, with two halfpence on each ear, to bee set out for him for his use, a year and a day after my decease.

I will and bequeath unto my grandchild, Mary Hunt, twenty shillings, to bee payed in a year and a day after my decease.

I will and bequeath unto my cousin, Johanna Burroughs, twenty shillings, to bee payed in a year and a day after my decease.

Furthermore I institute and appoint my beloved wife, Elizabeth Jessup, to bee whole and sole executrix, and I do will and bequeath unto her all my lands and houses, and goods and cattle, movable and immovable, of this my last will and testament, and to receive all debts, dues, and demands whatsoever, to be at her disposing, and she to pay all debts, dues, and legacies whatsoever, and she to bring up my two children in the feare of God. This I do owne to be my last will and testament.

Further, I do appoint my well beloved friends, Mr. Richard Cornhill, justice of the peace, Mrs. Sarah Bridges,

7

my well beloved brother-in-law, John Burroughs, and Ralph Hunt overseers of this my last will and testament, likewise to be assistants to my executrix in all cases and difficulties, and this I do owne as my owne act and deed, to all true intents and meanings, and doe, furthermore, ratify and confirm it as my owne act and deed by ye setting to my hand and seal, the day and year under-written.

August the 6th 1666.

Signed, sealed and delivered
in the presence of us, witnesses,
WILL'M GOULDSTONE, JOHN RICHARDSON,
mark of RICHARD HORTON, X.

JOHN I WHITMORE.

Died: Murdered by the Indians, October 1648.

Issue.

1. —— **Whitmore,** 1st wife of Edward Jessop, of Westchester, N. Y.
2. **Thomas Whitmore,** of Hartford and Middletown.
3. **John II Whitmore,** of Hartford.

Account of John I Whitmore.

1639 Owned land in Wethersfield, Conn. Resident of Stamford, Conn.

GENERAL BIBLIOGRAPHY.

Gen. Dict. of N. E.; Savage.
N. E. Hist. and Gen. Register. I. III. IV. VII. VIII. X. XIII.
Memorials of Marshfield; Thomas.
Hist. Sketch of Block Island; Sheffield.
Mass. Hist. Soc. Publications. 3d ser. VI; 5th ser. I.
Mass. Hist. Soc. Proc. II.
Records of the Colony of Rhode Island. I. II. III. IV.
Genealogies and estates of Charlestown; Wyman.
History of Long Island; Thompson, 2d edit.
History of Westchester; Bolton.
Annals of Newtown; Riker.
Comfort Sands' Manuscript Book.
A copy of the old epitaphs in the burying-ground of Block Island; Harris.
A History of the Bank of New York; Domett.
Chronological history of N. E.; Prince.
The town of Roxbury; Drake.
The Worcester Magazine and Hist. Il.
A gen. reg. of the first settlers of N. E.; Farmer.
Coll. of the N. H. Hist. Soc. IV.
Hist. of Marlborough; Hudson.
Biogr. sketches of the graduates of Harvard; Sibley.
Mass. Bay Records; Shurtleff edit. I. II. III. IV.
Hist. of Charlestown; Frothingham.